D1133227

RATTUS REX

The drainage of London is about equal in length to the diameter of the earth itself . . . The rat is the only animal found in the sewers.

H. Mayhew, *London Labour and the London Poor*, 1861

RATTUS REX

COLIN ANDREW M^CLAREN

REX COLLINGS LONDON 1978

First published by Rex Collings Ltd
69 Marylebone High Street
London W.1

© Rex Collings Ltd 1978

ISBN 0 86036 074 1

Typeset by Malvern Typesetting Services
Printed in Great Britain by
Billing and Sons Ltd
Guildford, London and Worcester

*To my daughter
Judith
who has heard it
all before*

Contents

I

The enemy advances

As the clock of St Anne's struck three on that cheerless November day, I wished myself Many Happy Returns, knowing that no one else would. It was 1863; sixteen years previously to the hour, I had been hauled into the world by the hags in the Soho workhouse and left to cry, while they had begun to lay out my dead mother. The occasion was duly recorded in the poorhouse register, together with the information that, my mother's name and father's where-abouts being unknown, the parochial guardians had named me Mathew Mark. They drew hopefully upon the apostles and evangelists when naming pauper bastards, but in vain: Peter Simon, my contemporary, was transported in '64; Luke James, my junior, was hanged last Christmas.

I peered out at the fetid court beyond the studio, where a sprat-seller trudged ankle-deep in scummy water from a dozen wash-tubs and thrust his way through garments draped on string between the houses. I almost envied him. He was free to go whither he chose, while I was bound apprentice to Pratt the engraver, with three years still to spend in drudgery, tracing in boxwood squares the crude lines and hatching of incompetent hacks. I had no illusions about the standard of our clientele. I fancied myself something of a draughtsman—two years under Mr Ruskin, I reckoned, would secure me a place in the Academy—and I had nothing but contempt for the artists we served. Not for us the Leeches or the Keenes; their work went to Dalziel or Swain. We, in contrast, dealt with little Lampiner of the *Illustrated Monthly*, to whom the rules of perspective were as the mysteries of the Masons, or with Hackett of the *Examiner*, whose last drawing of our gracious sovereign had

1

been considered by the few that saw it, tantamount to treason.

I craned my neck to observe, obedient to Mr Ruskin's writings, the small patch of sky visible above the tenements: a leaden pall of stratocumulus opacus. I sketched it upon a paper scrap. Pleased with the effect, I applied it to the drawing that I had been given to engrave, transforming sunlit manoeuvres on Salisbury Plain into anguished conflict under the shadow of death. My stool was hooked from under me and I sprawled upon the floor. Pratt my master stood above me, a mere five feet six but heavy with beefsteak and batter pudding.

'That's for wasting time,' he snarled, 'and this,' driving his boot into my ribs, 'is for a-tittivating of Mr Lampiner's drawing. It's not as if I haven't warned you often enough. Didn't I say that the next time it happened I'd kick you out for good?'

I chose this moment to shake my head, striving to clear it. He took the gesture for dissent.

'Call me a liar, would you? You insolent, ungrateful workhouse brat. Get out of here or I'll etch your behind with my graver.'

'Given your apparent incompetence with that tool, my dear sir, I don't think our young friend has much to fear.'

The speaker had entered unnoticed, a cadaverous giant in pepper-and-salt, with an eyepatch, who resembled no one more than the late President Lincoln in a ginger wig and whiskers. He loped across the studio and snatched up the offending sketch.

'The sky's not half bad. Too much Ruskin on an empty stomach, but it shows talent.' He rounded on Pratt. 'And you'd drive him into the gutter. I came here with a commission for you, sir, but hang it, I find you're a philistine.'

Pratt cursed his commission and damned his impudence, but the stranger ignored him and drew me to the door.

'Young man, if you intend to eat tonight, you've a choice to make. You can cringe your way back into favour here, you can entrust yourself to me, or you can turn thief. In all

2

fairness, I should say that you'll eat best by thieving; but if chops and a bottle of port will do you, I think I can offer you a way of life more suited to your abilities.'

Bemused by the sudden change in my prospects, I assured him that, compared with Pratt's meagre victuals, chops would be a banquet, and we departed. Pratt pursued us into the courtyard with an incoherent catalogue of crimes and a threat of litigation. My companion turned.

'Your premises contravene the Factories Acts on six counts, at least,' he asserted. 'And I have a friend in the inspectorate.'

We heard no more from Pratt.

My benefactor was Jabez Rimmer. Born on the bleak coast of Buchan and an alumnus of King's College in Aberdeen, he had drifted south into journalism and had eventually been accredited war correspondent to the old *Globe*. In this capacity he had survived a bout of cholera in the Crimea to write more bitterly of the horrors of the hospital at Varna than Russell ever dared. He had been a yard behind Havelock when the Highlanders charged at Cawnpore, had surveyed with Dunant the carnage at Solferino, and had studied Mandarin under the Taku forts. On the eve of the Civil War, he had talked strategy with Lincoln in the White House and with Jeff Davis in a Montgomery villa; then a Yankee bullet had hit him at Bull Run, and he had returned to England with an empty eyesocket. He had immediately raised subscriptions for an illustrated survey of life and labour along the Thames, which he issued in belated monthly instalments (hence his visit to Pratt), augmenting his funds with occasional pieces for *Punch* and the *Illustrated London News*.

All this I learned as we crossed Soho to Rimmer's rooms in Little Newport Street. They stank of tobacco and old books. I propped my pillow that night on first editions of Hakluyt, Camden, and Raleigh, bought for pence on the City Road stalls, and rested my feet on a shelf of geological journals. There were paintings, too, French daubs which I affected to despise; whereupon Rimmer damned me for a Ruskinite humbug and smoked three pipes while he spoke of *Réalisme*

3

and of bottles drained in the rue Lavoisier with a young artist called Manet.

Thus I became Rimmer's assistant, protégé or, when he felt expansive, disciple. I thrived on the life: a late breakfast of bread, cheese, and beer, a boat down to Limehouse Reach, and an assignation in a squalid lodging house or on a sagging jetty. Rimmer would put the questions, I would record the answers and, if requested, sketch the subjects. In a single day I might draw a mudlark, thick with slime at the water's edge; stand braced in a lighter to record the secrets of a tobacco smuggler from the Shadwell Basin; and hang from the gallery of a penny gaff to sketch a drunken waterman as he sang a comic song. Exhausted, we would return at night to dine on hot eels and pea soup at a stall in Windmill Street, and drink port with Rimmer's friends from *Punch*, Mark Lemon, Keene, Shirley Brooks and, when he wanted a low evening, Thackeray.

In moments of candour Rimmer would admit to some vices: a distaste for soap was one, a thirst for port another. To these I might add his jokes and his total lack of regard for Mr Ruskin and other eminent men whom I admired. As to his jokes, he earned small sums by concocting situations for Keene to draw in *Punch*, and was likely at any moment to nudge me, muttering, 'Here's one. Irish private: "Permission to speak, sor!" Irish captain: "Soilence when ye spake to an officer." ' My anguish, I believe, encouraged him. As to the ridicule to which my idols were subjected when the port flowed of an evening, it caused me considerable pain at first. How could I, who had gone hungry to buy *Modern Painters*, listen to Lemon as he chanted—

The dreariest thing about dreary old Ruskin
'S the prose that he scribbles from dawn until dusk in—

without championing the master? But at last I succumbed, suffering in silence while he, then Carlyle, then Mr Kingsley were savaged. Eventually I, too, would join in calls for Rimmer's 'Ode upon our Poet Laureate'.

4

Lord Tennyson, visiting Harrow,
Was wheeled through the school in a barrow.
It stuck in an aisle
And he said, with a smile,
'They build these damned crammers too narrow.'

For all his disdain of Mr Ruskin and my other heroes, Rimmer did his best to nurture my talent as a draughtsman and begged John Leech to help me. On evenings when Rimmer went to carouse at the Garrick Club, I would draw until my fingers throbbed, desperate for a word of praise from that gentle man who was dying slowly in Kensington Terrace, tortured by the unceasing noise from the street. One drawing of mine Leech admired above all: it showed the interior of a lodging house in Wapping, where, in a windowless room, under grimy walls that heaved with bugs, twenty lascars lay on beds of cotton flock in coarse canvas, pipes of opium at their sides. Leech showed it to his friend Frith, who said it was 'doocid hijus' but praised me highly; my encounter with the painter of 'Derby Day' was before long to save me from a beating.

On the morning of the first day of December, dark with cumulonimbus feebly lit from inside, Rimmer opened a letter, whistled at its contents, and tossed it to me. A Mr Jas. Lumley, styling himself Deputy-Chairman of the Metropolitan Board of Works, in effect the ruling body of London beyond the City boundaries, had invited my patron to attend a meeting at the Board's offices in Spring Gardens, near the Mall. The subject, wrote Mr Lumley, was one of great moment; too great, apparently, to be specified in the invitation. Rimmer attended, taking me with him in the role, as he explained to Lumley, tapping his eyepatch, of indispensable amanuensis.

While the first sleet of winter lashed the bevelled glass margin of the ceiling in the Board's council-room, Rimmer defied protocol by producing his pipe, and identified for me some of the other participants in the meeting: a senior official of the General Register Office; two principals from the Home Office; representatives of the Poor Law Board and

5

the General Board of Health; a quartet of superintendents from the Metropolitan Police; the chief officers of the Board of Works itself; doctors from the larger London hospitals; and parish clerks and vestrymen from the metropolitan parishes. What intrigued Rimmer most was the presence of a dozen men, all, like himself, accounted experts in London lore; he pointed to Mayhew of the *Survey of London Labour*, Timbs of the *Illustrated London News*, George Augustus Sala, and Knight of the *Cyclopaedia*.

Lumley's opening speech was brief but sobering. In the past three months, he revealed, London had been subject to an onslaught of crime of unparalleled proportions. The incidents had been scattered and had made no aggregative impact upon the public at large; but the evidence, pieced together by his officers and those of Scotland Yard, indicated a vast and growing menace, all the more fearful for its anonymity. He uncovered a map stuck with pins and invited a series of officials to provide statistics. The Fire Brigade was first, with figures of an unprecedented number of inexplicable fires; the Board's engineers were next, with an exceptional incidence of fractured and exploding gas pipes; the police followed, with a lengthening list of missing persons—solitary beggars who had vanished from streets, babies lost from perambulators, corpses taken from new graves. I felt pretty cold at the end of it all, and I noticed that Rimmer had not re-lit his pipe, a sure sign of concern. Lumley ended by explaining that he had taken the unusual step of summoning in confidence—he stressed the word—a wide range of authorities on the daily life of London, in order to invite explanations or theories of the source of so much evil.

They came—thick, fast, and fantastic.

'Chartists!' exclaimed a fat vestryman from Chelsea.

'Was necrophilia among the Six Points?' Rimmer asked.

'Fenians!' averred the parish clerk from Fulham.

'There were six Murphys, four Brannigans and a couple of Rileys among the missing persons,' Rimmer reminded him.

'Garrotters!' declared one of the doctors.

'Strangling gas pipes, I suppose,' added Rimmer.

6

He demolished a further half-dozen theories and Lumley became caustic.

'Perhaps our distinguished colleague has an explanation of his own,' he interposed.

'Possibly,' replied Rimmer, and sought permission to summon two acquaintances; he also asked for the unexplained fires, explosions, and disappearances of the past two years to be added to the map. Lumley agreed and adjourned the meeting until five o'clock. The sleet had stopped, so we went to eat sheep's trotters in Trafalgar Square.

When we reassembled, Rimmer's friends had arrived. He led the first of them, an elderly man in a black suit, viridescent at the seams, to the map now bristling with pins, and asked him if he could perceive in them a pattern. After prolonged study, the old man declared that he could: they were most dense where new sewers had been built, in particular along the lines of the new High and Middle Level intercepting sewers. Not an obvious conclusion, he added, but clear enough to a former clerk of the Sewer Commissioners.

There was a pause.

'I think,' said Lumley, 'that we should welcome the views of Mr Bazalgette, our Chief Engineer.'

I had once engraved Bazalgette's portrait for an article entitled 'The Saviour of London'; as he rose before us now, he diffused the strength and resolution with which he had tackled some of the most exacting feats of engineering of this century. Speaking in clipped, forceful phrases, he took us back fifteen years to a Thames of stinking, slimy water, swilling between foul mud banks the sluggish sewage of a hundred thousand drains, a source of noxious gases that spread fevers and, some said, cholera. He recalled the protracted series of Parliamentary Commissions and their abortive schemes for improving London's drainage; and he explained how, scorning their timid, tentative approaches, he had inaugurated his own system of drainage by driving vast pipes at right angles to the existing sewers, to intercept their contents and carry them off to an outfall many miles away.

Stepping to the map, he traced the line of the High Level intercepting sewer, from Bohemian Hampstead to respectable Holloway, that of the Middle Level sewer, from royal Kensington through corrupt Soho and shabby Bethnal Green, and pointed to their junction on the Hackney Marshes, whence they ran east to Barking Creek. The Low Level sewer, he added, would run alongside the Thames, and would be incorporated in the new embankment which he was building to deepen the river and quicken its flow, in order to scour away the mud.

'I agree,' he concluded, turning to Rimmer, 'that there is some correlation between the incidents and the lines of recent sewers, but I cannot account for it. Can you?'

'I think so,' replied Rimmer, and there was a buzz of expectation. 'Rats,' he said, and lit his pipe.

His thesis was simple, if incredible. When I asked him later how he had arrived at it, he gave a rueful grin.

'Not, I regret to say, by the methods of induction they taught me at college. I had spent the morning reading Southey; and when one of those policemen mentioned a fellow named Bishop who went missing near the Tower, I was put in mind of old Bishop Hatto and the rats. You remember?

> And up to the Tower their way is bent,
> To do the work for which they were sent.
> They have whetted their teeth against the stones
> And now they pick the Bishop's bones.

'It began a train of speculation which, of a sudden, seemed perfectly reasonable. I needed only a brace of knowledgeable coves to back me.'

Rimmer submitted to the meeting, that for time out of memory, rats had infested the sewers of London, living unmolested in these ready-made warrens, excavating and nesting amid the decaying brick and mortar of tunnels and channels that were, some of them, over five hundred years old. They fed upon animal and vegetable matter that had been swept into drains and gullies, or crept up at night to prey upon the houses above them. Then had come sanitary

8

inspectors and engineers who had destroyed the old drains and constructed new; more important still, Mr Bazalgette's gangs of men had gone to work across the entire metropolis. The rats had been dislodged and had retaliated against those who had invaded their territory, filling emptier bellies with their enemies' flesh and gnawing through their enemies' gas pipes in search of new warrens. A strange theory, perhaps. But investigations by historians and naturalists would readily show if it was supported by events of the past and by the known behaviour of rodents.

'Balderdash!' shouted the fat vestryman from Chelsea.

'Mr Browning has addled your brain,' sneered the clerk from Fulham.

'This is London, not Hamelin,' snapped the doctor.

'I am bound to say,' Lumley intervened, 'that I can scarcely credit the common sewer rat to be capable of inflicting such damage.'

In reply, Rimmer motioned forward the second of his acquaintances, a sober fellow wearing a broad strap engraved with the initials V.R. and the form of a rat.

'Mr Black, rat-catcher by appointment to Her Majesty the Queen, will, I trust, enlighten you.'

Didn't he just! He told us of a savage world, a teeming population, mere inches beneath us.

'Why, gennlemen, you take the Milford Lane sewer, a goodish bit afore you get to the Strand. I've seen 'ole rooms o' rats, great open spaces where the sewer 'ad rotted away an' the brickwork collapsed; an', leadin' off in all directions, tunnels into the walls; an' in each tunnel more nor a 'undred pair o' rats, rare big fellows, an' all their young 'uns, a-fightin' an' a-squeakin' away. Many's the time I've took to me 'eels, gennlemen, 'cos I knew I stood no chance agin' 'em.'

He spoke of sewer-hunters—toshers—searching in the slime at low tide, whose limbs had swelled like bladders from a single bite; of men buried under a mass of writhing, brown bodies and bitten to death.

''Tisn't ginerally known, but they'll go for children, the blood rats will; snake-'eads, we call 'em. I seen two babes

9

left in a cot that was gnawed to death, their little nightgowns all gory.'

As for gas pipes. 'I seen 'em gnaw through wood an' iron when they'd a mind to. There's that many, nothink'll stop 'em.'

The feeling of the meeting was still against Rimmer's theory, until a diminutive man with a nutcracker face spoke for the first time: Professor Richard Owen, Superintendent of the Natural History Department of the British Museum.

'I was invited here as a former sanitary commissioner for the metropolis, but I speak now as a scientist. Mr Rimmer's hypothesis, though strange, alone fits the available facts. His reputation as a journalist guarantees his abilities as an investigator. I move that he be empowered to pursue his theory further,' here Rimmer coughed loudly, 'at the Board's expense, of course, and with any other assistance he may require; and that he report back to this meeting with the utmost celerity.'

That did it. One did not lightly ignore Richard Owen. When Rimmer and I walked down the Mall that night, it was in the sobering knowledge that we had two weeks in which to prove his theory, a theory which, in the darkened street, greasy with sleet, took on a sudden, awful menace.

Back in Little Newport Street, we built up the fire, toasted cheese, and made plans.

'We need allies,' Rimmer announced, and extracted from an extensive acquaintanceship formed in an eventful career, the name of Wellesley Gunn, antiquarian. 'An Oxford man and a bit of a prig, but he quotes from the London chronicles in his sleep. I found him an Angevin charter once and he vowed me undying devotion.'

We also needed an expert upon rats. There was only one, Rimmer said, and, thank God, he knew him well: Donald McWhirrie, Professor of Natural History at King's College, Aberdeen.

'I soaked his venerable head in a riot once, but he took it like a sportsman, and I did penance by stuffing forty specimens for his museum. Creates a bond, that. He's a dour Buchan loon, mind. Can't see him taking to Gunn.'

10

The rest was simple logistics. While Rimmer went off to send telegrams, I hauled down *Bradshaw*. At dawn—ragged cumulus, brownish-grey—we were shivering upon the platform at Euston, awaiting the early train on the North Western Line to Bletchley Junction.

At Bletchley we changed to the Oxford Branch and, two hours later, stood beneath the groined gateway of Wykeham College, where Gunn was a Fellow. To our chagrin, the scout on his stair informed us that Gunn had left for the cathedral at Lichfield the previous day. Rimmer found beds for us with an Aberdonian at Balliol and the next morning we travelled to Rugby, thence by the Trent Valley to Lichfield. I was cold, tired and aching when we entered the cathedral close that evening, and my temper worsened when we learned that Gunn had disappeared into the cathedral roof. We climbed fifty feet to find his plump form, in neatly-fitting black, wedged upon a beam from which he was tracing carved initials. Our unexpected arrival dislodged him from his perch; and his comic reappearance from the beam beneath, crowned with cobwebs, dissipated my foul mood.

Gunn gave us dinner in the close and, when we had feasted on cold fowl and the canons' first-rate port, Rimmer explained the reason for our visit. The antiquarian's response was emphatic.

'My dear fellows, a pleasure to assist you. Indeed, had you denied me the opportunity, my regret would have been immeasurable.'

He left for London the following morning, '. . . to discover, if I can, an historical basis for your theory,' and promised to meet us in six days. Two hours later, we travelled north.

As we steamed towards Stockport, I continued to enjoy my first excursion into provincial England, darkened now under blue-grey nimbus; but Rimmer was glum, telescoped in his seat, chin deep in his greatcoat, wrestling in silence, I assumed, with the problem of the rats. I was wrong, as I discovered when our engine ran into the rear of a dozen wagons and jumped the line. Rimmer brightened.

'There,' he said, emerging from our carriage, which had

11

lurched into a ditch. 'I've been waiting for that to happen. Never travelled with a company yet that could keep its stock on the rails.'

He cheered up sufficiently to nudge me later and mutter, 'Here's one. Second-class compartment full of old women. Policeman and prisoner at door. "Come on ladies, give him a hand. He can't help himself with the cuffs on." Consternation!'

A cold hour passed before we travelled on a replacement train through Manchester and Preston to Carlisle; thence, after a dreary Sabbath, by the Caledonian to Edinburgh. At the Waterloo Hotel there, a telegram from Aberdeen awaited us. McWhirrie was in Orkney. There was nothing for it but to commandeer the clerk's *Bradshaw*, where we learned, to our relief, that we had an hour in which to break our fast before the *Prince Consort*, the weekly packet from Granton to Kirkwall, raised steam. We were bundled aboard with four minutes to spare and collapsed upon the deck, heedless of the purser's warning of a gale and high seas. Two very sick men peered out at Kirkwall Bay the following morning.

It was on the tiny isle of Burray, a rattling cart-ride and a dismal boat-trip away from Kirkwall, that we ran our quarry to earth—literally. Deep in a Pictish broch, crouched a very Pict of a man, stringy frame wrapped in a disreputable plaid, wizened face under a grubby bonnet, peering at droppings on the frozen ground. Professor McWhirrie chuckled over the memory of Rimmer's student escapade and gave us a hearing. His eyes brightened at the mystery and, when Rimmer had propounded his theory, he thumped his thigh and cackled.

'Man, Rimmer, ye're a credit tae the college, nae mistake; an', forebye, I think ye've the truth o' it.'

'Will you join us?' asked Rimmer.

'Haud on, haud on,' cried McWhirrie. 'Ye're owre hasty for a Buchan loon.'

'We have to leave Kirkwall this evening,' I explained.

McWhirrie communed with himself and poked distractedly at the earth. Then: 'Aweel, mebbe,' he muttered.

That, I discovered, was the nearest he came to an

12

affirmative. Yet taciturn and dilatory though he might be, on the subject of rats he was inexhaustible, speaking with the authority of one who held honorary doctorates from universities in Austria, Prussia, and France. Seventy hours with him on boat, train, and coach made us authorities too; and when we were back in Little Newport Street I was scholar enough to annotate every line of the article on 'Mammalia: rodentia' in Rimmer's *Britannica*.

Gunn had installed himself with a maiden aunt in a riverside house at Hammersmith, which was crammed with relics of bellicose Gunns who had died in Sinde and Kabul. It was thither we went the next day, under globulated masses of stratocumulus, to hear his report. Most of his time had been spent in the Public Record Office and the British Museum, where the messengers had measured his consumption of manuscripts by the hundredweight. His sources had been varied: the annals of a Thameside priory, a Tudor merchant's diary, Roundhead newsbooks, and the burial registers of a dozen parishes. They all told of marauding rats; and by diligent investigation he was able to link many of the incidents to the construction of ditches and earthworks. The prosaic McWhirrie, who, from the outset, had irked and been irked by the plump and pompous don, wriggled with impatience throughout Gunn's recital. Now he broke in.

'Man, a' this is scarcely relevant ava'.'

'Not immediately, I admit.' Gunn was huffed. 'But I have made a more pertinent discovery, if you would care to hear it.'

Rimmer soothed him. 'We are all attention, Gunn. Aren't we, McWhirrie?'

'Imph,' said the professor, 'mebbe.'

Gunn read from a sheet of blue foolscap:

From the minutes of the Sewer Commissioners in the City of London, 12 December 1664.
Whereas it hath been represented to us by divers memorials of householders, that rats hath at many times wasted their stock and assaulted their children, whereof some have died; resolved that all constructions and workings of new sewers shall cease, for that such workings do aggravate the beasts.

13

He paused. 'The sequel, gentlemen, was . . .'

'The Plague!' I cried, 'in 1665.'

Gunn nodded. 'Then came the Fire in the following year, which presumably destroyed many of the rats, enabling the City commissioners to proceed with their new works.' He tapped the sheet. 'There, gentlemen, is an undeniable link between the aggression of rats and the construction of sewers.'

Gunn's aunt brought in tea. McWhirrie exclaimed in delight at her home-baked scones; charmed by his praise, she invited him to lodge in the house, and to Gunn's dismay the professor accepted. We returned to the rats; and McWhirrie announced that he was unimpressed with Gunn's researches.

'There's mair tae the current seetuation than a wheen beasties bitin' some bairns,' he declared. 'An' I'm thinkin' the cause'll no' be foon' in buiks but in Nature.'

It was now Saturday, the twelfth. A useless Sunday and a Monday remained before we were to report back to the Board of Works, and it seemed impossible that McWhirrie would discover his natural cause in the time. But on Monday evening he burst in upon us—we had assembled again at Hammersmith—crammed a buttered scone into his mouth and told us that he had succeeded. He had visited the menagerie in the Zoological Society's Gardens and there had overheard an attendant discussing with a passer-by the nature of the animals. All, the man had said, were quiet now. Now, McWhirrie had queried. Had something been amiss with them? Why yes, the attendant had replied. They had all been taken queer after the earthquake.

We stared at each other. Why had we not thought of it before? On 6 October, England had been shaken by an earthquake. London had felt a tremor of no more than thirty seconds, but that, as the attendant revealed, had been enough to terrify the animals in the menagerie. Camels had smashed their stalls; apes had torn up railings; and, in the aquavivarium, alligators had threshed at their tanks until the glass had shattered. But it was among the docile burrowing mammals that the effect had been strangest and most prolonged: there had been no rats to observe, but jerboas

14

and chinchillas had run wild, snapping and biting until none dared approach them.

'An' there ye hae the answer,' McWhirrie concluded. 'A' yon biggin' doon in the sewers sair worrit the rats and sent them stravagin' owre the toon. But it was the earthquake pit them in a panic an' set them at oor thrapples.'

We had been asked to report not to the Board of Works but to the Home Department; and on Tuesday Rimmer and I arrived punctually in Whitehall—nimbus above, full of grey rain—carrying a report over which the four of us had laboured all night; my role had been that of scribe, Rimmer's of general editor and custodian of the peace, whenever Gunn had derided McWhirrie's laconic style or McWhirrie Gunn's verbosity. We were taken to the room of a senior official, Mr Ashley Durston, and it was under his quizzical eye that Rimmer reaffirmed my indispensability. Lumley from the Board of Works arrived next, together with Bazalgette and Richard Owen, and reported that the other theories canvassed at our last meeting, Chartists, Fenians, and garrotters, remained unsubstantiated; he hoped that his distinguished colleague and er—(the 'er' was me) had brought better news. He added that, since the matter had been placed within the competence of the Home Department, he would with pleasure resign the chair to Mr Durston, and did so.

Durston looked youthful and a trifle languid, but Rimmer found out later that he was thirty-six and had been a Senior Wrangler at Cambridge. He was dressed with faultless style—I had engraved enough advertisements for morning and evening wear to perceive first-class tailoring when I saw it—and he displayed the same taste in the adornment of his office. Rimmer remarked later that Sir George Grey, the Home Secretary, would have an apoplexy were he to see the Rossetti and the Holman Hunt that hung above his subordinate's mantel; he added that he himself did not care for the works but admired the gesture.

Rimmer read his report; Bazalgette and Owen nodded approval as the thesis was developed, Lumley frowned incomprehension, and Durston's eye wandered to the

15

Rossetti. Yet the official's attention was fully engaged, as his summation showed.

'You argue, then, that sewer rats, which in the past habitually responded aggressively to interference with their environment, have, as a result of the recent tremor, acted with especial ferocity in the last three months, attacking helpless humans and damaging subterranean installations.'

Richard Owen asked a question. 'If the mammals at the Zoological Society's Gardens have returned to a normal state, why not the sewer rats? The number of outrages shows no sign of diminishing.'

'Certainly not,' Durston interposed. 'Each occurrence is now reported to this office and their incidence has, in fact, increased.'

'My colleague, McWhirrie,' explained Rimmer, 'believes that panic would subside more rapidly among a few animals in captivity, with a regular food supply, than among a vast, wild population. He says also . . .'

A messenger knocked and delivered a note to Durston, who glanced at it and rose.

'To our hitherto circumstancial evidence, gentlemen, we may now, perhaps, add positive proof. A further outrage has occurred. But on this occasion there is a witness to its nature.'

II
We reconnoitre

The rain had turned to sleet as our cabs scurried across Westminster to Drury Lane. A constable met us there and conducted us through a labyrinth of alleys to Perseverance Place . . .

'Where it 'appened, gennlemen. Low neighbour'ood this but you'll be all right with me. They know me 'ere.'

He proved his boast by cuffing a way for us through the crowd that had gathered in the mean court, and guffawed as it parted sullenly before him. A deep crevasse had opened in the ground, causing the last of a small terrace of houses to topple forwards into it. This sometimes happened, Bazalgette explained, after hard frosts, in slums where houses had been built without proper foundations over forgotten cesspools, burial pits, or vaults. The front of the house had already subsided, taking occupants and contents with it; the back, side and sagging first floor still hung over the pit.

'Been like that this past hour,' said our constable and suddenly thrust us backwards. With the sound of rending timber and grinding stone, the rest of the house collapsed; rubble filled the hole and brimmed over its edge; and Durston looked with dismay at the plaster that settled upon his boots.

'Them dahn there is past diggin' fer,' observed a costermonger.

'Poor divils,' chorussed the crowd.

'Two wimmen an' their brats,' a labourer took up the litany.

'Poor divils,' came the response.

Our constable winked at us. 'We 'ave a witness,' he said,

'as reckons they've already bin made orff with. Over 'ere, gennlemen.'

The witness was an old Irish dame squatting against a wall, grisly hair hanging in matted hanks about her withered face. The constable hauled her up.

'Tell 'em what you saw,' he ordered.

'Nuffin',' she whined. 'Leave me be.'

A young woman hurried to her side, glared at us and snapped, 'Send that bully away, he terrifies her.'

Durston dismissed the policeman and the young woman soothed her charge. 'Come on, Mrs Lynch, you're not in any trouble. Just tell them what it was that you saw.'

Mrs Lynch did not look up. 'Dogs,' she muttered. 'Couple o' dogs an' some puppies.'

The young woman explained that when the ground had given way, everyone had been watching a fight two streets distant, save Mrs Lynch, who had been hanging washing in the yard, and the occupants of the house, a mother in labour, a friend and their children. When the subsidence had ceased, Mrs Lynch had looked over the edge of the hole and had seen the bodies of the women and children lying crushed and twisted. She had called to them but they had not moved; then she had seen animals moving about at the bottom of the pit.

'Dogs.' The Irishwoman spoke. 'Like terriers they were. Nivver seen 'em come. The big 'uns tore into them carcases, pulled orff arms an' legs an' bit 'em into pieces that the little 'uns carried away. Seen it, I did.'

She lapsed into mutterings and the young woman took her into a house.

Lumley broke the silence. 'Dogs, Mr Rimmer? Are the outrages, after all, caused by stray dogs?'

The sleet turned to snow and we sheltered under an arch.

'Well, Rimmer?' Bazalgette was grim. 'Dogs or rats?'

'I still say rats. McWhirrie believes that we may be dealing not just with vast numbers of the brutes, but with a strain of exceptional strength whose size might well be that of a small dog.'

Lumley looked unconvinced, but Owen came to our support. 'I've read somewhere of a *Mus giganteus* from

18

India, Malabar I think, which is over three feet in length and weighs several pounds. Rodents are clearly capable of such extended growth.'

Bazalgette snorted. 'Then the sooner we exterminate them, the better.'

Durston nodded, asked for forty-eight hours in which to consult his superiors, and departed. Lumley and Bazalgette followed. Rimmer and I were left contemplating Perseverance Place.

A woman spoke behind us. 'Kindly tell me what is happening?'

It was the protectress of Mrs Lynch, a majestic creature, whose name, we learned, was Miss Emily Tiptree; her wrathful appearance, however, so reminded me of a picture of an outraged beauty which I had once engraved for little Lampiner, that I habitually called her by its title, Pride and Passion. She had, it appeared, caught the end of our conversation and now demanded to know its significance. We temporized.

She smiled. 'My uncle writes leaders for *The Times.* Perhaps I should refer the matter to him.'

We remonstrated. She prepared to depart. We capitulated. Whereupon she conducted us to a nearby religious and medical mission to which she was attached as a nurse. She had trained, we discovered, in the Nightingale School and devoured its founder's *Notes on Nursing* as eagerly as her Bible.

'And what is going to happen now?' Pride and Passion asked, when Rimmer had finished his account.

'We'll know that in two days,' he replied. 'But whatever we decide, it must be kept a close secret.'

'Don't you think these poor people have a right to know what is occurring?' she demanded.

'Miss Tiptree,' Rimmer emphasized every word, 'if talk of the rats spreads, there will be panic throughout London. And it will be your "poor people" who will suffer most.'

'I don't see . . .'

Rimmer silenced her. 'Once I was in a Chinese port when plague was discovered. The mandarins left by litter. The

19

poor were forced to tear with their bare hands a way through the cordon of soldiers that guarded a departing ship; but when they tried to scramble aboard, sailors leaned from the deck to chop at their fingers as they fumbled for the rails. Humans are ugly, Miss Tiptree, and at their ugliest when they are frightened.'

'Fiddle!' replied Pride and Passion. 'Miss Nightingale, I'm sure, was never more lovely then.'

Rimmer smote his head in despair. Pride and Passion produced another of her infuriating smiles.

'Very well, Mr Rimmer. I shall hold my tongue. But on one condition. That I be allowed to join you . . .'

'What could you . . .' Rimmer began but this time was himself silenced.

'If nothing else, I can see that the poor people in St Giles and beyond have someone to speak for them when you make your plans. Your word, sir, or I go to my uncle.'

'My word,' Rimmer affirmed; and, when we were trudging back to Drury Lane, 'My word!' he exclaimed. 'What a frightful young woman. I'll send a note to Durston. Wait until he meets her.'

We talked late with McWhirrie and Gunn and were breakfasting, torpid, in Little Newport Street the next morning when Durston appeared. There was snow upon his collar and, from the look of the slate-hued cumulus above, more was due. He whisked us off at once to Westminster where, he explained, there was unrest among the labourers working on the new embankment along the Thames and in the Low Level sewer.

'Unrest', translated, meant a strike that threatened to become a riot. It had begun a week earlier when Selina Smith, a gipsy given to much-publicized predictions, had settled among the labourers. Within forty-eight hours she had terrified them. At night, when torches flared around the camp filling the hollows with shadowed menace, Irishmen with fearful eyes had listened as she told them of the mysterious Thames, an age-old stream that would brook no tampering with its course. The day its banks were bound with stone, she had declared, it would rise and spew forth rats to

20

stalk its defilers and gorge upon their flesh. Had it not already begun its revenge? Were there not even now strange happenings in the city, folk that vanished, corpses too?

A coincidence? Durston wondered. Or had someone from our circle talked carelessly? The elderly clerk? Mr Black, the rat-catcher? Rimmer was doubtful. The old man would not jeopardize his pension; and as for Black, if Her Majesty trusted him, why shouldn't we?

'But I don't believe in coincidence either,' he growled, 'or crystal spheres. That old gipsy can read the papers. She's guessed at the truth. And she's tried it out on those likeliest to listen, navvies and sewermen.'

Listen they had, Durston affirmed. And when Selina's voice had ceased and they had heard in its place the sinister suck of the current at the shore, they had believed her. Hundreds had queued to buy amulets blessed with her power, the only sure protection against rat-bite. Their fear had survived the morning light but not their belief in Selina's amulets; instead, a deputation had waited upon Furness, the contractor for the works, demanding that he protect the site with traps and poison. He had refused. The men had struck. He had resisted. They had threatened to burn his equipment. He had lost his nerve; and Bazalgette, as supervising engineer, had been asked to intervene.

'Mr Bazalgette felt, quite rightly,' Durston explained, 'that he could not interfere with the rats until our plans had been laid. He is with the men now, trying to calm them.'

As we left our cabs near Westminster Bridge, it was clear from an angry roar that Bazalgette was trying in vain. He was surrounded on the embankment site by some three hundred men who shivered in the snow flurries; more clung to derricks, timber and mounds of ballast, and still more to the vast iron caissons that loomed over the site, ready to form the coffer-dams behind which the embankment would rise. Some carried picks and staves, others hefted stones, and many called for a march upon the Board's offices. A cordon of constables was settling its helmets and fingering its truncheons. Durston saw it. His habitual languor vanished and he hurried to join Bazalgette, beckoning to Rimmer to follow.

21

'I know you have a turn for humour,' he said. 'Let us put it to good use. Only laughter now will stop a battle.'

As they disappeared into the throng, Rimmer shouted back to me, 'Get it down on paper, boy, even if they tear us apart. *Vive le Réalisme, hein?*'

He always spoke in French when he felt heroic.

I perched upon some balks and started to sketch. So intent was I, that I did not notice the ring of men that had closed around me.

'Police spy,' said one.

'Gittin' of our descriptions,' cried another.

''Ammer 'im,' bellowed a third and lunged at my legs.

I toppled backwards from my perch; the balks impeded my assailants and gave me a start. I needed it. Rimmer's late nights, his port, and his tobacco had impaired my wind. They were gaining on me as I turned into Whitehall and when I collided with a bulging topcoat, I rebounded from it directly into their grasp. They wrenched my arms up behind my neck, grabbed at my flailing legs, and fumbled for my sketch-book. The topcoat spoke.

'Drop him, Pierce, there's a good chap.'

My arms were released and my principal antagonist blushed under the kindly gaze of Frith the artist.

'Your daily exercise is your own concern,' he remarked, 'but one of the boy's boots might have blacked your eye and, damme, you're modelling for me tomorrow.'

''E were spyin' on us,' muttered Pierce, 'a-takin' av our descriptions.'

'Bosh!' exclaimed Frith. 'I know the lad. He's an artist like me. Making another of his hijus sketches, I'll wager. Here!' he tossed a coin, 'quench your thirst. And turn up on time tomorrow.'

The men grovelled. Frith walked me back to the embankment. As he left me there, he remarked that there was a time and a place for sketches from life; if I misjudged one, I would not long enjoy the other.

The site was still crowded, but the atmosphere, I noticed at once, had changed. Rimmer and Durston were emerging from the mob amid good-natured jesting and boisterous

22

laughter. They looked pretty pleased with themselves.

'Hang it,' cried Rimmer, 'Mathews himself couldn't have done better.'

'My dear fellow,' replied Durston, 'your true vocation is burlesque.'

They had, I learned, appeared at Bazalgette's side just as the mob had surged towards him, and had caught its attention only by bellowing that its demands were to be met. In the moment's silence that had followed, Durston had added, 'We always act upon Miss Smith's prophecies.' Whereupon they had recalled several of Selina's predictions and had held them up to ridicule.

'Foretold the winner of the Derby Stakes last June, I believe,' an innocent Rimmer had remarked.

'Indeed she did,' a solemn Durston had replied. 'And the Chancellor planned to halve all taxes with his winnings.'

'Why didn't he then?'

'Damned nag's still running.'

Laughter rippled. So they had attributed some new prophecies to the gipsy, each more scandalous than the last. The men had loved it, had participated, and had called for more. At which point Bazalgette had stepped in to show them how near they had come to making prize fools of themselves and had gone into conference with their leaders.

'I got away with a single concession.' Bazalgette joined us, accompanied by a bandy gnome. 'Told 'em we were investigating all the disappearances and agreed to take one man of their own choice into our counsels to protect their interests. Here he is, Mr Tom Scud, who turns out to be not only a shrewd debater but a former sewer-hunter—a tosher—into the bargain. Why, he knows his way underground as well as . . .'

'As Ai knows the insaid av a bottle,' finished the gnome. 'Pleased tew meet yees, sors.'

Durston sighed. 'Yesterday Miss Tiptree. Today Mr Scud. Pray, gentlemen, resist the temptation to extend the alliance further before tomorrow's meeting. The Home Office is desperately short of chairs.'

Bazalgette and Durston departed and Rimmer led Scud

23

and myself to a stall that sold, he vowed, the best Yarmouth prawns in London. While we ate, Scud entertained us with his autobiography. He had starved on black potatoes in a turf hut in Ireland as a boy and had taken ship to Liverpool to escape. Thereafter, he had shifted earth for Stephenson, driven rivets for Brunel, and climbed scaffolding for Paxton. Now, after two years spent hunting for valuables in the sewers, he was tunnelling for Bazalgette. His reminiscences were interlarded with quotations which meant nothing to me, but which Rimmer identified as Malthus, Mill, and Bentham. Tom Scud, he said later, was better read and had more sense than most of the windy orators of his race.

When Scud had finished, Rimmer summarized recent events for him. In response, Scud asked if we had been down into the sewers and when we replied that we had not, looked puzzled. Rimmer explained that we were eager enough to explore them but lacked good maps and feared to trust a guide lest he should betray our secret.

'Ai'll take yees,' said Scud.

'When?' asked Rimmer.

'Now,' said Scud.

So we went.

Scud recommended a trial run through the Covent Garden sewer, entering from the new subway in King Street. From a swag shop we procured canvas aprons, leather hats with neck guards, high boots, gloves, and a bull's-eye lantern apiece. Then we walked to the subway, a great, vaulted passage under the recently-built street, which housed all the necessary water and gas mains for the vicinity and from which a manhole led into the sewer. We were admitted through a side entrance after Rimmer had mentioned Bazalgette's name and a coin had changed hands, and descended some seven feet by rungs to find ourselves in a tunnel just over five feet high, along which we stumbled to the subway, where we could stand upright once more—all but Rimmer who cracked his head on the roof and swore. From here we dropped through a manhole into the sewer itself. Not into impenetrable darkness as I had imagined, but into the murk of an unlit chapel on a winter afternoon. The sewer was four feet high

24

and under three feet wide. Scud and I crouched without much discomfort but Rimmer was painfully contorted. Even when we had gone further and had gained an extra foot in height, his blasphemies continued.

'Obsorve the walls,' advised Scud. 'Trai tew remember each daitail; 'twill help if yees lewse yer way.'

'What happens when a man is lost?' I asked.

'Can't say. Nivver knew one as was found.'

His answer intensified my concentration and I began to memorize the features of each section: iron girder, cracked at joint; bricks in shape of fish; recess; drain choked by rubble; broken arch, two stones missing; manhole marked 9 . . . and so on. The mental effort not only banished any fear of losing my way, it made me less conscious of the stench. Bearable when we had entered the sewer, this had thickened as we progressed, and now enveloped us, so that we inhaled it, tasted it, saw it steam from the tide of sewage, and felt it settle upon our skin. Scud alone was unaffected; he swore that toshers thrived on it, that all his mates had been 'well set-up an' rosy'. As we waded through the sewage, my bull's-eye glinted upon its strange flotsam of pots, chains, cutlery, branches wreathed in slime like outstretched arms, and coins—the last in such quantities that I remarked upon them to Scud, saying that the toshers must have had an easy living. Scud shook his head. The dangers of falling, of being caught by tides or unexpected flushings, he explained, made sewer-hunting a risky business. To say nothing of the rats.

Indeed, we had said nothing of the rats since entering the sewer, for the simple reason that we had seen none. The drains and gullies seemed uninhabited. I said as much to Scud, who laughed.

'They're about us shewr cnough. Jist dew as Ai dew and listen.'

We walked on twenty paces. Then Scud froze in mid-stride. As we balanced, motionless, we heard them behind the brickwork: not the delicate patter of scampering feet but the steady beat of lithe-limbed beasts running down their prey. Scud saw the fear in my eyes.

'Aisy, lad,' he smiled. 'They won't attack us while we're

fresh and fearless. Taired men, scared men—that's their prey.'

A quarter of a mile farther, Scud stopped us again. We had seen, he said, a main sewer; now he would show us a branch. He ducked under an arch and the ceiling closed in upon us again so that we walked almost upon our knees. I tried once more to memorize the features of the walls but the brickwork was old and crumbling, stained green and black by spreading fronds of filth. The darkness was deeper, the sewage thicker, the stench more vile; and I felt the tremor of pursuing rats, mere inches, it seemed away. Then Rimmer stumbled, lurched against the wall, and the bricks gave way before him. He disappeared through a gaping hole; there was a slither followed by a dull impact. Scud scrambled into the aperture and withdrew quickly.

'There's a divilish drop. He's gone straight down. We must get tew him before the rats.'

We directed our lanterns through the wall and saw that Rimmer had broken into a stone-faced shaft that led to a lower tunnel. There were enough crevices in the masonry to enable us to descend hand over hand, and in this way we covered some fifteen feet, breaking our final drop upon Rimmer's crumpled body which straightened under our boots as its owner expressed himself in a bout of comprehensive cursing. He was bruised and lacerated and had lost his eyepatch, but he revived quickly to ask where the devil we were. Scud had no idea, and offered to investigate.

Before us lay a tunnel even narrower than that which we had left. Scud threaded himself into it but promptly retreated. It had long been in disuse, he told us, and its structure was dangerously rotted. Rimmer, still recumbent, examined the brickwork with his bull's-eye. Under their crust of blackened matter, the bricks of the lower part were clearly different from those of the upper. They were smaller, squarer, and deeper in tint. On one Rimmer found some scratchings that he read as MDCXXII, and began to theorize.

'Open drains for a Cavalier's house, perhaps? Roofed over by his grandchildren? Forgotten and built over by

26

theirs? Gunn says that there are hundreds of miles of disused drains under London, unknown or unmapped.'

'Sor!' It was Scud, agitated. 'Look there!' He flashed his lantern into the shaft above us. Trapped momentarily in the light was a great, pointed muzzle; in it huge incisors were bared in a snarl and behind it massive shoulders were hunched. It was our first sight of the enemy. A snake-head rat as big as a boar. McWhirrie had spoken of large rats, but this was a giant.

We doused our lights, dropped to the ground and squirmed into the narrow tunnel.

'Let's hope it leads somewhere,' muttered Scud who went first.

'Anywhere so long as it's away from that fellow,' prayed Rimmer who followed.

I said nothing, fearing at every second to feel the brute clawing at my heels. We covered thirty yards then Rimmer stuck. There would have been some humour in the sight of that ungainly torso worming and squirming, had the horror of our recent encounter not been upon me. But I was conscious only of the heightening temperature in the tunnel, of the perspiration that streamed into my eyes, and of the acrid odour of my fear. With a convulsive heave Rimmer freed himself, but no sooner had he drawn his heels forward than the sides and roof of the tunnel bulged inwards and collapsed. When I had scraped the dust and earth from my face, a wad of brick and stone sealed me off from my companions. I tore at it until my gloves were shredded and the tips of my fingers bled, but I could not dislodge as much as a single brick. I thought of the tons of earth, paving, and masonry above my head and fancied that it bore down upon me; a moment later I fainted. When I recovered consciousness my nostrils, eyes, ears, and mouth were clogged with dirt. I vomited and lay weak and shivering. I knew then that I must withdraw from the tunnel into the shaft and face its sentinel before my strength was finally dissipated. The retreat seemed endless and ever in my ears echoed Scud's words, 'Tired men, scared men, that's their prey'. At length, however, I felt a draught of cooler air and

27

thrust myself out into the shaft.

I rose, each muscle locked and sore, and shone my bull's-eye upwards. To my relief the rat was not at the rim. But as I bent to scrape some of the filth from my clothes, I felt a weight upon my back and claws raked my leather neck-guard. I arched my shoulders backwards and, by striking the wall of the shaft, dislodged my attacker, a rat only a little larger than normal. As it squeaked and rolled away from my lunging boot, I felt the impact of more upon my shoulders and, snatching a glance up into the shaft, I saw a dozen leaping down towards me. My face was unguarded and my hands, too, where I had torn my gloves. Jerking and weaving my body to shake the beasts loose, I ripped off my scarf and muffled myself to the eyes; then, balling my fists and windmilling my arms, I retreated to the wall of the shaft again and, by rubbing against it, scraped the brutes from my shoulders. When I sensed that I was free of them, I thrust out from the wall and kicked and jerked, while they withdrew across the shaft and faced me in a semicircle, whipping their scaly tails from side to side with a hypnotic force that I found hard to resist. I dragged my eyes away and upwards once more and saw the great muzzle loom above the rim. It gave a raucous call and I sensed that the beat of the tails around me had accelerated. When I looked again at the rats, movement convulsed them entirely, their bodies writhed in unison. Rimmer had told me of savages who danced themselves into a frenzy before attacking; I believed these animals were doing the same. I searched in desperation for some means of defence and, as I did so, felt a slight motion in the stonework behind me. I groped and found that mortar had fallen from between two slabs of facing and that I could prise one of them loose. Ammunition! I knew now that I could at least put up a decent fight.

With intense care I transferred the slab to my front, expecting at every moment to see the writhing cease and feel the shock as the creatures flew at me. Yet at length I held it there, ready to smash it upon them. The raucous cry came once more from above and the rats stopped their motion; but even as I tensed and waited for their spring, I heard a whistle from the tunnel, looked towards it, and saw Scud there, beckoning. I waited no longer, but flung my slab at the rats; it shattered against the opposite wall and fragments spurted amongst them with stunning force. I threw myself at the tunnel's mouth and Scud shunted me into it; then he knelt and, with airy unconcern, catapulted a hail of stones upon the rats that had survived my slab, smashing their frontal bones with such force that they dropped without a jerk or quiver. As he turned to join me in the tunnel, I trained my light upon the rim of the shaft for the last time. Aghast at what I saw, I motioned to him to look. The sentinel still gazed down upon us; but in his eyes we saw not the blank fury of a beast baulked of its prey; instead, there was menace, malevolence, and a hate that was not animal at all, but human.

As we stared, I felt a stab in my arm. A stunned rat had revived and was clinging to me, its teeth fast through my sleeve and into my flesh. Scud snapped its neck and pursed his lips.

'Ye must have that wewnd traited at once, son. Down the tunnel, now. There's an aisy way out at the end av it.'

He explained as we went that, while Rimmer had torn down the blockage, he himself had explored the tunnel and had found that it opened into the Long Acre sewer, one he knew well. But by the time we had rejoined Rimmer and were thrusting forwards again, I was no longer able to take in their exploits. Fiery pain pulsed along my arm until it felt like a bar of glowing metal. I fainted and only recovered when Rimmer hit my head a cruel smack on the rim of the manhole through which we clambered to fading daylight.

Scud insisted on taking me at once to his home in Shoreditch; his wife, he said, had grown used to treating rat-bites. The cab swayed and jolted, sending waves of pain along my arm. I felt Rimmer's arms around me and heard a soothing voice; then I fainted again.

When I came to, my arm had been bathed and poulticed with herbs; I felt cool and clear-headed. I thanked Mrs Scud, a dark, wiry woman from whose skirts peeped dark, wiry children, and looked about me. The room, though small,

29

was airy; the floor was as white as if it had been newly planed; crockery shone upon a dresser; and the wall was patched with pictures of Scud's heroes cut from the illustrated papers. (I spotted two of my own engravings).

Gunn and McWhirrie had arrived on Rimmer's instructions. Having overcome a certain pique at their exclusion from our expedition, they asked how I did and, before I could reply, what I had seen. I told them, shuddering as I recounted the fight in the shaft. Gunn fastened upon the disused tunnel: it was in such, he believed, that the large rats bred, which explained why they had not hitherto been noticed in the main sewers. McWhirrie, in turn, concentrated upon the behaviour of the rats that had attacked me, and made me repeat several times the precise sequence of their actions and those of the giant rat.

'My opeenion,' he averred at length, mouth filled with Mrs Scud's strong tea and soda bread, 'is that ye saw a war band and its laird. Yon auld wumman in St Giles mebbe saw the same. I've studied the social organization o' these beasts; there's nae doot at a' that the big yins are the war-lairds, the ithers jist dee their biddin'; they carry aff the meat an' dee a' the fechtin'. Tell me, ma loon,' he swallowed his mouthful, 'did they mak' a muckle din?'

'No noise at all,' I replied; and as I spoke, I remembered the words of Black the rat-catcher, 'a 'undred pair o' rats a-squeakin' away'.

McWhirrie nodded as he saw my expression change. 'Aye, jist so. Nae skirlin', jist the yin cry fae the leader. Man, d'ye no' see? They're tae keep quiet so's he can gie them their orders. They've learnit discipline. We're no' dealin' wi' naturally independent brutes; we're dealin' wi' an army.'

At Little Newport Street, a note from Durston informed us that our venue the next day would be the regimental headquarters of the Queen's Royal Rifles in Kensington.

Rimmer sniffed. 'I might have known. Confront the Home Department with an unprecedented situation and they refer it to the Army.'

His exasperation was exacerbated when we arrived at the Rifles' barracks, its roof smartly trimmed in fresh snow

30

under bleary stratocumulus. We were passed from one disdainful being, braided and befrogged, to another and were eventually left to kick our heels under a wallful of battle-standards and trophies.

Rimmer was unimpressed. 'It's not a regiment I admire,' he said.

Had he, I asked, had previous dealings with it.

'In the Crimea, when I was a correspondent. Went foraging with one of their sergeants when we ran into a Russian unit that should have been snug behind the walls of Sebastopol. Instead, it pinned us down for six hours.'

His eyes narrowed as he relived the experience. The Russians had been in no hurry; they had known that they could make the kill when darkness fell. The sergeant, meanwhile, convinced that he was done for, had talked freely to Rimmer of his regiment and its ways—ways so brutal that Rimmer, not a squeamish man, had paled. An Arab slaver, he had decided, was an angel of mercy compared with the young sprigs who had commanded the Rifles. Then a troop of dragoons had taken the Russians from the rear and Rimmer and his sergeant had stepped to safety over the cloven skulls of their enemy.

'But,' sighed Rimmer, 'like the young fool I was, I taxed one of the Rifles' officers with the stories I had heard. Didn't say who my informant was, but the officer—a Captain Augustus Crashaw, rot him—found out, and submitted the poor fellow to every torment and degradation that Queen's Regulations permitted, with a few that they didn't. When I saw the sergeant again, he was a private, broken in mind and body, who spat in my face and wept that he had not died under the boulder.' Rimmer drew a breath. 'No, it's not a regiment I admire.'

My questions were forestalled by the appearance of Durston who ushered us into a council room. Owen and Bazalgette, Scud and Pride and Passion—Miss Tiptree—sat around an oaken slab. At its head were two men. The first, a ripe plum with white whiskers, rose as we entered. I had engraved enough portraits and caricatures of him (one much resembled the other) not to need Durston's announcement:

31

'Lord Yelverton, Undersecretary of State in the Home Department.' The second man was in uniform, his features indistinguishable against the window of watery sun; but as he too rose, I felt Rimmer stiffen. Durston continued to do the honours.

'My lord, may I present Mr Rimmer and his—er . . .'

'Amanuensis, indispensable amanuensis,' Rimmer prompted.

'His amanuensis. Mr Rimmer, may I introduce the officer commanding the Queen's Royal Rifles, Colonel Crashaw.'

'I am acquainted with the gentleman.' The edge in Rimmer's voice left no doubt as to his antagonism. Crashaw tightened a peevish mouth and fretted with the discoloured whiskers that straggled beside it. Durston, aware of a hostility that he could not comprehend, hurried to hand us agendas.

Rimmer was called upon to narrate our exploits underground. He paid tribute to Scud's resourcefulness, causing the latter to blush brightly, and summarized the theories of Gunn and McWhirrie. When he had finished, Pride and Passion looked critically at my bandaged arm, but I gave her an inane grin to assure her that it was mending. Mrs Scud's poultice might not have come out of *Notes on Nursing*, but I did not intend that Pride and Passion should set to work on me with swabs and disinfectant. Owen and Bazalgette questioned us closely and conceded that Gunn and McWhirrie had drawn the correct conclusions.

Lord Yelverton listened impatiently. At length he interrupted.

'It's all rather academic. I have attended this morning solely to give notice that the matter is now in the hands of the Army. Since the skill of sharpshooters seemed called for, it has been entrusted to Colonel Crashaw. He has already outlined to me a plan in which I have every confidence. It will require no further,' he sneered, 'investigations of a scientific or journalistic nature.'

Silence. Then Pride and Passion responded. 'The colonel's plan will not, I trust, endanger the working populace?' She treated Yelverton to one of her smiles. 'The Army is not noted for consideration in its dealings with the common people.' Good old P. & P.

Crashaw flattened her. 'I can assure the young lady, though I was unaware that her presence here was other than as an ornamental observer, that my plan is simple and free of all danger to the inhabitants of the metropolis, whatever their estate.'

'What do you propose?' asked Owen.

'A shoot,' replied Crashaw. 'We shall declare open season upon rats, drive 'em through the sewers and pot 'em as they run.'

'You'll send Riflemen into the sewers?' Bazalgette was incredulous.

'My dear fellow,' Crashaw waved a negligent hand, 'not Riflemen. No need for that. There are excellent Volunteer companies in London. Always crying out for rifle practice. I shall send them. I propose to arrange a trial run a night hence.'

III
We join battle

'I need fresh air,' declared Rimmer. So we splashed through the slush to Kensington Gardens. 'If I'd stayed in there any longer, I'd have beaten Crashaw over the head with one of his own rifle-butts. The pompous, opinionated imbecile.'

I remarked that in the Imbecile Stakes Yelverton was an equally strong contender. We had argued with them for three hours: Rimmer heatedly, Owen forcefully, Bazalgette bluntly, and Pride and Passion so doggedly that Yelverton had forgotten his manners and had cursed Miss Nightingale and all her brood. But we had achieved nothing. Only Scud, politely questioning the logistics of Crashaw's operation from his intimate knowledge of the sewers, had shaken the colonel; at which point Yelverton had been quick to terminate the discussion with the instruction that Scud, Rimmer, and I should hold ourselves in readiness to offer such information or assistance as Crashaw might further require.

We ate at a fried fish stall and Scud appeared, breathless, at our side. 'Lord, it's a great pace ye go at. Ai thought Ai'd nivver catch yees.' He refused a hunk of smoking haddock. 'Sor, ye must stop yon sojer. Thim Volunteers'll not stan' a chance below.'

Rimmer tossed his fishtail to the robins. 'It's out of our hands, Scud. Didn't you hear his lordship?'

Scud damned his lordship. 'If Ai'da left young Matt here down the sewers as aisy as ye're washin' yer han's of thim lads, what wud yeesa called me thin, eh?'

Rimmer made no reply, but I took the point. 'You must do something,' I cried, sadly aware that I lacked Mr Gladstone's eloquence. 'You'll feel awful after if you don't.'

Six furious feet of Rimmer, crowned with a ferocious eyepatch, towered over me. 'Confound your impudence! Telling me what I'll do and what I'll feel.' He thumped my skull. 'Can I not implant in the remote fastness of what passes for your brain that I—we—are powerless? When you fight the Yelvertons and Crashaws of this world, you find they're invincible.'

'But you're not fighting,' I persisted. 'You haven't even begun to fight yet.'

Rimmer swore. 'Faced with an obstinate brat like you,' he snarled, 'I perceive the greater wisdom of King Herod.' Then he grinned and it was like the sun bursting through in one of Mr Turner's skies. 'But hang it, you're both right. Very well. Back to Little Newport Street. McWhirrie and Gunn will be there. We'll hold a council of war.'

Pride and Passion was there, too, having begged our address from Durston. She was folding away unasked the garments that bedecked the room. Rimmer scraped out his pipe over her neat pile of linen and re-enacted the meeting for McWhirrie and Gunn. Another visitor, Durston, arrived.

'Er, I am not here in any, er, official capacity,' he explained with unwonted hesitation. 'Merely to suggest on behalf of Messrs Bazalgette and Owen that a further approach to Colonel Crashaw under more propitious circumstances might yet be fruitful.' He addressed himself to Rimmer. 'We feel that the grudge between you and the colonel reinforced his natural tendency to obstinacy. If you were to renew your persuasion, first offering to redress whatever grievance irks him, he might be sufficiently mollified to accede to our remonstrations. Once Crashaw has been dissuaded, Yelverton will quickly succumb.'

Durston when embarrassed spoke like a Blue Book. Rimmer when enraged did not. 'Damn it all, I said I would help. But I'll not crawl before Crashaw. The man's a fool, a bully, and a hypocrite.'

'Mr Rimmer,' it was Pride and Passion. 'I came here to beg you to renew your arguments against the colonel. I see now that I must do more. I must ask you to set aside your honour and that is to demand much of a man. I would not

35

ask it, did I not speak for many poor folk who will suffer from this day's work.' She didn't spoil it by gulping or dabbing her eyes but sat up straight and looked at him. There were times when you just had to admire old P. & P.

We waited for McWhirrie to swell the chorus but instead he rose. 'I'm awa' hame tae ma bed,' he declared. He struggled into his coat but paused at the door, revealing that he too had a sense of the dramatic. 'I'm an auld mon, wi' nae thochts o' honour an' the like, but I ken this: till noo we've aye spoken o' thae rats as beasties. An army, aye, but beasties nanetheless. Yet d'ye min' fit the loon,' he gestured to me, 'said the ither day aboot the luik in yon gran' rat's e'e? Nae that o' ony beast but human. Aweel, I'm thinkin' that's aboot the size o' it. See, these rats hae livit wi' man for centuries; they've watchit him fae their wee neuks; an' they've seen his cruelty, his lust, an' his evil. They've learnit it a' fae him. It's ma belief that in yon strain o' big rats, the war lairds o' the warren, intelligence has come tae replace instinct. Intelligence as cruel an' calculatin' as oor ain. An' on their ain grun', in the sewers, they're fair unbeatable. Thae sojer-loons hae nae chance. Noo, I've said ma piece. I'm ga'in'.'

Rimmer rubbed his pipe against his nose. 'All this preaching. Like a damned revivalist meeting. Hang it, I'm converted. Durston, what must I do?'

The following morning found Rimmer and me crossing Parson's Green in Fulham under a sky heavy with snow-filled cumulus. Crashaw was there, attending the man-oeuvres of the West London Volunteers, and Durston had told us that this would be an opportune time to catch the colonel. He delighted, it seemed, in the sight of fat clerks and market-gardeners from the suburbs of Fulham and Hammersmith shivering under rotting canvas and fumbling with blue fingers at obsolete weapons. When the parade had been dismissed to the cookers, we asked to see him. He was addressing the captains of the Volunteers on the turn-out of their companies, supported by two junior officers from the Rifles, who neighed in unison at his flights of sarcasm.

'It will be of great consolation to my Riflemen, gentlemen,

to know that, should they fight alongside the Volunteers, the efforts of your gallant fellows will swiftly render the enemy helpless—with mirth.'

Seeing us, he dismissed his hapless butts and with an ill grace asked our opinion of his geese. 'Soon to become swans, d'ye think?'

'Soon to be slaughtered,' was Rimmer's reply.

Crashaw flushed. 'I trust that you don't intend to waste my not unlimited time with further irrelevant objections to my plan. I have already enlisted the aid—eagerly volunteered, I may say—of these brave fellows here. They shoot a dozen rats a day on their market-gardens and along the riverside.'

'But have they hunted them underground?' asked Rimmer. 'Have you told them of the giant breed?'

'Giant breed,' scoffed Crashaw. He pointed to me. 'A fancy bred in the wandering wits of that moon-faced lout or the inventions of your trouble-making Irish radical. I'll hear no more of them. Now take yourselves off and report for duty as guides to my rat-hunters at nine o'clock this evening in the Hammersmith drill hall.'

'Well, we tried,' said Rimmer and led the way back across the green.

The drill hall at Hammersmith was the size of a young cathedral and as cold. It was empty when Rimmer and I arrived in foul tempers, having spent the afternoon in attempts to persuade Durston to make a last appeal to the Undersecretary, only to find that his lordship had fortified his sanctum with a triple ring of secretaries, each with orders to refuse Durston admittance. The cathedral doors slammed; Scud approached us through the gloom and inspected our appearance. Crashaw had ridiculed his suggestion of protective garments for the Volunteers—'Breastplates and helmets as well, Mr Scud?'—but the former tosher had dared us to appear without gauntlets over our hands and arms, waders to mid-thigh, leather jerkins buttoned to the throat, and caps with neck-guards. The doors slammed again and Crashaw with his staff stamped into the hall, brushing off a sprinkling of sleet. They were followed by a company of one hundred West Londoners, who paraded and numbered off in fives. Rimmer looked in disbelief at their weapons.

'Muzzle-loading Enfields! Where does Crashaw think he's sending them, Salisbury Plain? What will they do at close quarters?'

Scud pointed in reply. From each belt hung a truncheon. The War Office, which habitually starved the Volunteers of decent weapons, would not even stake them to a hundred hand-guns.

Last to arrive was a wagon, which disgorged a gang of ruffians, each one as diminutive as Scud and each as stoutly garbed. Beside them, the Volunteers with their plump, green-trousered calves, looked overweight and vulnerable. The newcomers were toshers, Scud told us, recruited, as we were, for guides.

Crashaw mounted a dais to address the men and announced their objective, which, we gathered, he had merely adumbrated at the time of their recruitment. They were, he said, to clear a single sewer of rodents: the Covent Garden sewer, to be precise. If the exercise proved successful, and he was sure that it would, the method would be applied to the other principal sewers of the metropolis in order to solve a pressing, but not serious, nuisance. The West Londoners, therefore, stood to add lustre to their already not inconsiderable reputation by their pioneering efforts.

'Hang it,' moaned Rimmer, 'they believe him. Look at their smirking faces.'

Each squad, continued Crashaw, would cover a single section of the sewer, hunting and exterminating the rats in its gullies, drains, and branches. Their task completed, the men would leave by an appointed exit and would report back to field headquarters at St Paul's, Covent Garden. He paused and coughed, and I waited for him to mention the giant rats, the war-lords as Rimmer and I now called them, but instead he muttered something about luck and a good haul, saluted, and left the dais. His opinion of the Volunteers was clearly so low that he deemed it neither necessary nor advisable to warn them of the nature of their adversaries.

The company fell in and marched through flurries of snow

to a jetty by the suspension bridge, where a vessel was raising steam; we followed with the other toshers on the wagon. Touching new depths of ineptitude, the force took thirty minutes to embark and when, on a final command from Crashaw, the paddles churned, the steamboat nosed its way gingerly into what had become a blizzard.

Rimmer had, as usual, insisted that I should sketch what I could of the evening's adventures and I began to draw my squad as it stood grouped at the deck-rail estimating its bag for the night. There was Corporal Bunce, whose paunch quivered over his breeches as he took bets on the highest count; his particular cronies were the wizened Private Winser and the pallid Private Sweetlove; beside them stood Private Gilshinan, who smoked a cutty and spat with an easy grace into the ice-crusted river; and at his shoulder was the sad-eyed Private Gotto, who ceaselessly cracked his long and bony fingers. As the group broke up in sudden commotion, I looked up to find that we had reached Westminster and were approaching a makeshift jetty near the caissons of the new embankment. Chelsea, Battersea, and Vauxhall, snow-blanketed, had slid past unnoticed. The Volunteers formed up and disembarked, excelling themselves by taking only twenty minutes to do so, and we set off for Covent Garden.

We saw few people as we marched through London that night; the blizzard had driven them into steaming kitchens and airless parlours; and even the homeless had scrambled from the roads to huddle in black alleys around glowing mounds of rubbish. We followed the line of the sewer, halting at intervals while a squad fell out, levered off a manhole cover, and descended into the section allotted to it. My squad stopped at the entrance to the King Street subway and I led it along the familiar passage with that sense of impending doom that every novelletist inflicts upon his hero in the penultimate chapter. I could have done quite well without it.

Our descent into the sewer was halted by Corporal Bunce, who stuck like a stopper in the manhole; we popped him through at last, however, and he reasserted his authority with terse commands to his men to poke into every drain and gully. Fifteen minutes . . . thirty . . . passed, but they found nothing. Periodically I stopped them and listened. The rats were there all right, well-hidden behind the brickwork; I could hear the occasional scraping of feet or tails. Then, when we were midway along our section, there came a raucous cry and I felt my stomach shrink. Somewhere a war-lord had taken command and the rats were on the offensive. At once they began to emerge, peeping from the mouths of branch-sewers, just out of range.

'Right, lads,' gloated Bunce and sent Winser and Sweet-love at the double into the nearest inhabited entrance. We heard shots and crows of delight and Winser reappeared with a brace of brown bodies bouncing from his fist.

'Sweetlove's got a 'undred bottled up in a gully at 'is mercy,' he announced. 'I'll go an' 'elp 'im finish 'em orff.'

'Not if it's that easy,' said Bunce; and he told the men to take a branch apiece. 'You,' he turned to me, 'stand by an' keep count. I'm goin' up beyond the next bend, see what's a'ead.'

The men darted to the right and to the left and I was left alone, comforted by the sporadic reverberations of their gunshots; but soon these ceased and I heard only the gurgle of the sewage. My palms grew wet. Sweetlove, at least, should have cleared his gully and returned by now. I went to his branch and shone my bull's-eye into the mouth but saw nothing. I called out to him, but there was no answer. I ducked, entered, stumbled forward twenty paces, and checked. Something glinted in the sewage: the barrel of an Enfield rifle. I turned a corner and saw its owner. Sweetlove lay slumped in the filth, mantled by a gorging brown mass.

I backed into the main sewer and ran after Bunce. I stopped, reassured, when I saw him ahead, crouching in the stream, one hand clenched upon his truncheon. But as I drew near, the truncheon fell from his grasp and he toppled forwards into the slime. Shapes detached themselves from his collar and swam to the edge of the channel, leaving the sewage at his neck curdled red. I stooped over him and saw that his throat had been torn out.

As I rose, retching, a bullet chipped the wall behind me.

Winser was teetering in my direction, rifle loose in one hand, Gilshinan's pipe clenched in the other. I shouted to him to stop, but he reloaded and fired again and a bullet scored my jerkin. I called once more as he drew abreast but he stumbled past me. His eyes were rolling, his jaw was slack and mewing cries of protest bubbled through the saliva at his lips. Whatever he had witnessed of Gilshinan's end had left him demented. Reloading once more, he took thirty steps farther; he tripped; there was an explosion; and by the time that I had reached him, he was dead from the bullet that had pierced his temple.

I heard a long, unbroken scream and seconds passed before I realized that the voice was mine. I blundered along the sewer, changed direction at a junction and, lost, slid helpless to the ground. There I squatted and held my throbbing head until a ripple in the sewage aroused me. Arrowed heads were surging in my direction and I sensed movement along the sewer's sides. I made no attempt to defend myself; the knowledge that the suspense was at an end, and that there was no escape, left me curiously tranquil. When Rimmer, Scud and a group of soldiers crawled from a branch-sewer to my right and dispersed my attackers with a smart volley, I was almost resentful of the interruption. Then I started to shake, and remember no more until I found myself gagging on the neck of Rimmer's whisky-flask.

I had one horror yet to endure. For as Rimmer drew from me a fragmented account of the fate of my squad, I saw that a soldier held a body in his arms. The head lolled and I pushed past Rimmer for a closer look.

'Found him layin' in a gully at the end av a branch,' said Scud. 'Is he one of yours?'

I nodded. It was Private Gotto. But where his sad eyes had been there were bloody sockets, and the long, bony fingers were jagged stumps.

'We lost our way chasing and being chased by the rats in the branches,' said Rimmer. 'But Scud thinks there's a manhole somewhere near here.'

We covered a mile, however, before we found one, the Volunteers turning and firing every fifty yards or so, to hold off the pursuit. As we went, Rimmer told me that both his squad and Scud's had, like mine, been decoyed and separated; they, too, had heard the cry of a war-lord. Reviewing the sequence of events, Rimmer began to speculate.

'Once the rats saw what we were up to, they must have devised a counter-plan. Our fire-power together was too much for them so they tackled us singly. Divide and rule. It's just as McWhirrie says, they've studied us and learned their lesson well.'

We halted under the manhole and Rimmer, whose authority the Volunteers had tacitly accepted, sent Scud—'He's the nimblest'—up the score of metal rungs that led to it, in order to free the cover. Our pursuers settled fifty yards away and watched us in silence; hearing splashes, however, I shone my bull's-eye around and saw a file of the brutes crossing by ledges above our heads and dropping to the floor behind us. We were surrounded. From the rear of the main band came the now familiar, raucous cry. The rats began to flick their tails and to writhe in unison, preparing to attack. A series of clangs, interspersed with Irish imprecations, told us that the manhole cover was rusted tightly in its socket. Then:

'Praise be, 'tis givin' a paice.'

There was a screech of metal and Scud dropped to the floor in a shower of dirt and a draught of icy air.

''Tis off,' he said.

The effect upon the enemy was instantaneous. Their writhing ceased and their backs arched.

'Look!' I cried.

Thrusting forwards among them were the massive shoulders and bristling muzzle of a war-lord. I heard his cry and the mass rippled towards us.

'Fire!' shouted Rimmer, and the Volunteers' Enfields blew a gap in the first rank.

'I'll swear I 'it the big 'un,' said one of the West Londoners, 'but 'is 'ide's that tough 'ee nivver noticed it.'

While the rats hovered, momentarily irresolute, Rimmer set me upon the lowest rung below the manhole and ordered two Volunteers to follow.

'Don't argue,' he snarled as I protested. 'Never met a man yet who'd let himself be saved without a fuss.'

My boots, caked with filth, slipped upon the metal, but when I paused to secure my footing, I heard a second salvo below and over it Rimmer's bellow, 'Hurry, damn you!'

I started upwards again and clambered at last over the rim to sink face foremost into thick snow. I rolled upon my back and shrank in dismay under the gaze of a blackened skull. When the Volunteers emerged and pushed me aside, I found that we were on the edge of a churchyard and that the skull was of weather-worn stone, marking the grave of Caleb Webster, *obiit* 1820. Looking beyond it, I saw a church of unmistakeable design and realized that in our wanderings we had strayed from the parish of St Paul, Covent Garden, into the sewers of the parish of St Pancras.

There was a muffled explosion from the manhole. Two more Volunteers surfaced and reported that the rats were ready for the kill.

'Then Rimmer's going to need these,' I cried, and made for the church wall, where I had spied scaffolding, ladders, and rope. We were almost too late. When we returned, the last Volunteers were hauling themselves over the side of the hole, badly bitten about the legs; they said that Rimmer and Scud were hard pressed and that only their stout clothing was saving them from fatal wounds. There was no time for ladders. The men tossed one end of the strongest rope into the shaft and wound the other around a tree, while I hung sacking over the manhole's edge to prevent the rope from fraying on the metal rim. There was a sudden glare from the hole, a rapid fusillade, and the rope was jerked hard. The men heaved upon it and Rimmer and Scud rose to the surface, clasping one another around the line like miners ascending from a pit, their garments smouldering and their whiskers singed.

As the Volunteers replaced the manhole cover, Rimmer and Scud lay gasping on the snow. At length, they explained that when the rats had finally rushed them, Rimmer had wielded a noble truncheon, while Scud, scrambling up the

43

rungs below the manhole, had taken from his pocket a ball of tarry yarn and matches. Just then, our rope had dangled in the shaft and, calling to Rimmer to shake off his playmates and lay hold of it, Scud had ignited his ball of yarn and had flung it straight at the war-lord, burning his muzzle raw before he could douse it in the stream.

'And that scared them off?' I asked.

'That and the thirty cartridges stuck insaide the ball,' grinned Scud. 'They couldn't tell where the nixt bang would come from.'

The trick, he added, was called 'the toshers' last resort'; you used it only when a charred nose was preferable to a chewed one.

The snow had stopped, but after our sojourn in the sewers we found the cold intense. The Volunteers danced and slapped their arms around their chests, jigging so vigorously that they seemed to make the gravestone near them shake. Then they stopped, and I saw that the slab continued to quiver. The others caught my look of horror and followed my trembling finger. The stone was slowly rising, borne on massive, singed, and blistered shoulders, while a stream of dark bodies squirmed through the widening gap and out on to the snow. We stared about us: a dozen graves were open and a circle of rats was tightening upon us.

Clubbing our rifles and swinging our truncheons, we burst through the perimeter, ran for the scaffolding upon the church wall, and climbed from it to the portico of the adjoining vestry. When we were safely aloft, Scud demonstrated the expertise he had acquired as a scaffolder on the Crystal Palace by quickly demolishing the poles and trestles. Kneeling behind the caryatids, terracotta maidens that bore the heavy portico upon their heads, the Volunteers fired at the rats who swarmed across the snow to leap and claw for a grip upon the smooth Portland stone of the vestry wall beneath us. The parish of St Pancras snored through it all; the wind had risen and it whirled the sound of our shots away, high above the chimney pots of Bloomsbury. At first we cursed it, but when it bore towards us the first flakes of a renewed snowfall we stopped. For even as the Volunteers reported to Rimmer that they had only one round left apiece, we heard the war-lord's cry—low-throated this time, less of incitement than of reassurance—and, when we peered from behind the caryatids' skirts, we saw the line of rats recede until the blizzard curtained them from sight.

Half an hour later we presented ourselves before Crashaw, who sat hunched at a desk in the vestry of St Paul's Church, grey about the mouth, his eyes dark with strain. Ours was the last, and the worst, report. He had lost, he admitted, twenty men and ten more were likely to die from infected bites.

'And what will ye tell their families?' Scud lunged over the desk in fury. 'That ye sacrificed their husbands and fathers by sendin' 'em where no sojer should 'a' bin sent? That ye tewk not a blind bit av notice av all ye was told?'

Crashaw rose and walked to the window. He stared at the snow outside that gleamed purple in the coloured glass.

'Next of kin will be informed that the lives of the men were lost when a case of ammunition exploded during a subterranean exercise; and that no bodies were recovered. A letter of condolence has already been drafted and has received Lord Yelverton's full approval. I will not detain you further. Good night, gentlemen.'

We did not move. He turned upon us, his mouth tight.

'They were only market-gardeners playing at soldiers. From the military viewpoint, the only viewpoint, they were expendable.'

'What will you do when the seventy survivors and the guides give their own account of the business?' asked Rimmer.

Crashaw purred. 'I think you will find that the generous compensation the men are to receive for their trouble will ensure that their stories will agree with ours. As for the guides, all of them are suspected of criminal offences; the threat of gaol will shut their mouths.'

Rimmer made a final effort. 'And suppose we go to the newspapers with our story?'

'They will print what we tell them. Furthermore, Lord Yelverton has made an interesting, unofficial disclosure concerning the government's new tax proposals. It will more than occupy the editors' interest.'

Rimmer gestured in despair and Scud and I followed him from the church. Outside, the blizzard had worsened and we trudged through heavy drifts to Little Newport Street, taking Scud with us as the roads to Shoreditch were blocked.

'They'll retaliate. The rats'll tak' their revenge and God kens faur.' McWhirrie stumped about the room. He and Gunn had awaited us in our rooms and had revived us with hot toddy and baked potatoes. Now we watched him glumly from the fireside. 'Fit hae a' these incidents been but retaliation by the rats agin oor deesturbances o' the sewers?' he continued. 'Wi' the cunnin' they possess, I'm feart tae think fit they'll dee next.'

'Wherever they go,' Gunn arched his plump fingers, 'they will seek food.'

He was right. The late editions of the following day's *Times* carried a report of a mysterious disturbance in a large warehouse beyond Blackfriars, which catered for the trade in animals—not domestic dogs, cats, and tortoises but large, wild animals, destined for circuses and menageries. It had occurred early in the morning. Animals awaiting collection by their buyers had stampeded. No one knew why. They had attacked the attendants who had been turned out to pacify them. One man, struck by the razor-edged hoofs of a plunging zebra, had been killed immediately; another, buffeted by the paw of a bear, had been torn to death as he writhed, impaled upon bars that had been wrenched from their sockets and twisted into a cluster of lances by the trunk of a newly-imported elephant; portions of a third had been found, some time later, submerged in a fetid tank that contained a hippopotamus. Others had been bitten by lizards and snakes. A noted zoologist, called in to advise, left three fingers in the mouth of a camel, whose docility had made her a firm favourite among the crew of the vessel that had trans-shipped her. Many sacks of animal feed in a store adjoining the warehouse, the report added, had been damaged and depleted, although by what agency was unknown.

We knew well enough and our expected summons to an emergency session of what we now called 'Yelverton's

46

committee' came soon afterwards. The meeting was called for six. In the meantime, Rimmer sent me out into the sleet showers that had succeeded the snowstorms for food and drink (we had neglected the larder in the past few days). He had, he declared, a taste for curried mutton, and dispatched me to a Hindoo merchant who kept a barrow in the New Cut Market of Lambeth.

'Met him in the Mutiny. Capital fellow. Tried to cut my throat, so I broke his jaw. Now he sells me first-rate spices at a discount, for old time's sake.'

I had just bought a dozen screws of oriental powders from Rimmer's chum and was pushing my way back through the heaving, shoving mob of shawled wives and shabby working men, sweating under the glare of gas lamps, grease lamps, and guttering candles, when I noticed a familiar figure. It was Durston, sheltering under a tattered awning that covered a counter of deal sodden with fish-ends, and talking to a barrel of a man whose face, too, seemed familiar, although I could not at once identify it. I was puzzled. Civil servants, I knew, even those of Durston's seniority, must occasionally shop for food, when their men were sick or their house-keepers away; but his stylish coat and boots were more appropriate to Jermyn Street than the Cut, and I imagined that his taste would have run to delicate soles rather than rank haddock. Pondering the problem, I collided with a print-seller, his umbrella turned inside-up and full of his wares, which I strewed over the pavement. By the time that we had retrieved them from the slush, Durston and his companion had vanished.

At six o'clock Rimmer and I were shown once more into the council room of the Rifles' barracks. Yelverton was in the chair and Crashaw sat at his right hand, his mouth a little tighter than usual but otherwise apparently unaffected by the fiasco of the previous night. Of the rest of the committee, only Pride and Passion was absent, inexplicably.

Yelverton allowed no time for recrimination. 'As a result of our recent experience,' he announced, 'Colonel Crashaw has had the opportunity to reformulate his scheme for the clearance of the sewers'; and he invited the colonel to speak.

'It's simple enough,' said Crashaw, 'I shouldn't have entrusted the job to those damned civilians in uniform. Incompetent lot. We need tougher material. I'm not going to waste good Riflemen, however. Convicts, those are what we'll use. Offer 'em remission for services rendered.'

'Her Majesty's Commissioners for Prisons have been approached informally,' continued Yelverton, 'and are in wholehearted support of the measure.'

There was a crack. Rimmer's fingers, tightening in anger on his pipe-stem, had broken it. 'Are not the lives of thirty poor lads from Hammersmith enough for you? You cannot, you must not, use inexperienced men for this work.'

'I see no reason to prolong this discussion.' Yelverton pushed back his chair and rose.

Scud, leaning across Rimmer, ignored the chairman. 'In God's name, sor, if ye cannot be persuaded tew forego the aidea, at least give thim pewr divils a dacent chance.'

'What do you suggest?' Crashaw was cautiously interested. Scud was the only one of us whose judgement he respected.

'Flush the sewers with water first, sor. 'Tis the way we've killed sewer rats in the past. Why can't we dew it now?'

Yelverton referred the question to Bazalgette. The engineer frowned.

'Simultaneous flushing on a comprehensive scale is impractical. We haven't the men to do it. But local operations, in the Covent Garden district for example, can still be mounted. We have discounted the idea hitherto, in view of the danger to the flushermen. But we'll try if you like.'

'We should all be grateful if you would,' said Rimmer, and Owen grunted assent.

'I've no objection,' added Crashaw, 'provided that it does not involve any postponement of my exercise. I have planned it for tomorrow night.'

Bazalgette said that he would set his department to work at once and the meeting was dissolving almost amicably when a Rifleman entered, saluted and passed a message to Crashaw, who shared its contents with Yelverton and Durston. The

Undersecretary cleared his throat.

'Our enemy is on the attack again. In the vicinity, it would appear, of Miss Tiptree's dispensary. This note is from her. She would welcome your assistance, Mr Rimmer.'

When Pride and Passion called, it was a bold man who withstood the summons. Cabs were fetched. Yelverton carried Crashaw off for further discussions with the Prison Commissioners; Owen and Bazalgette departed for the Engineering Department of the Board of Works; Rimmer and Scud set out for St Giles in one vehicle, and I found myself sharing a seat with Durston as we followed them in another.

Beyond a languid nod, Durston had made no attempt to acknowledge my presence at any of our past meetings. Now he sat aloof in one corner while I occupied another and sought for a gambit with which to open a casual conversation.

'Do you often go to the Cut?' It was the best I could do. 'Rimmer says it's the finest market in London.'

An eyebrow arched to denote incomprehension.

'The Cut. You know, the market in Lambeth. I saw you there this afternoon.'

'Then,' remarked my companion, 'you were evidently the victim of an hallucination.'

'But I *did* see you,' I insisted. 'You were talking to a man.'

'Hallucination,' came the reply. 'The apparent perception of external objects not actually present.'

I was young and not over-endowed with intelligence, but I had good eyes and believed the evidence of them. I leant back in my corner and wondered why Mr Durston should tell a lie.

IV
Counter-attack

Our cabs deposited us at Pride and Passion's mission, a dingy, single-storied hall of liverish brick, at the door of which were clustered a dozen crones carrying bibles. The mission fulfilled its dual religious and medical purpose, we discovered, by insisting that applicants for medical aid should first attend a Bible class. We found Pride and Passion in the dispensary at the back, rolling bandages and packing them in a bag with salves and disinfectants. Where, we asked, were the rats? She had a pin between her teeth and merely pointed through the barred window. We looked, and saw a huddle of lights a hundred yards along the road. Pride and Passion finished her preparations and led us out of the rear door. As we drew near to the lights, I saw that they were held by some two hundred people who were massed at the edge of the road, supervised uneasily by a constable. I had never seen a crowd so still and asked Pride and Passion the reason.

'You'll see,' came the grim response, and a moment later I did.

The crowd was peering down into a trench nearly fifty feet deep, the sides of which were boarded with planks and lined with scaffolding. A notice-board beside the trench announced that a subsidiary entrance to the Middle Level sewer system was under construction by the Board of Works. The site was fenced, but at one point the barricade had been flattened. In the trench below lay the wreckage of an omnibus and beside it two dead horses. Men with lanterns were rummaging among the splintered timbers of the vehicle, calling softly to each other. I heard the same word again and again: 'Dead'.

50

'There were thirty children in the omnibus,' said Pride and Passion, 'from poor families. The mission had arranged a Christmas treat for them. Just as they were leaving, an urchin threw a snowball and frightened the horses. They bolted, slid on a patch of ice, and the whole contraption careered through the fence and into the hole.'

'And the rats?' asked Rimmer.

'The children were trapped in their seats; they were shocked, but none was badly hurt. The men shot the horses—they'd broken their legs—and told the children to stay quiet and they would fetch ropes and ladders. At first we heard the children laughing and singing; then came screams; we couldn't see what was happening but one voice cried in fear, "Rats, ma, rats!"'

'And then, ma'am?' Scud prompted her after a pause.

Pride and Passion swallowed. 'When the men returned to the bottom of the pit, they found that the children nearest the door of the omnibus had been bitten to death. That's when I sent for you. They've only just broken through the timbers into the front part. I brought my bag in case any there were still alive but . . .'

'The rats had squeezed through where the men could not,' Rimmer finished.

Pride and Passion nodded.

'Were the bodies mutilated?' It was Durston, pale, his langour gone.

The reply came from the first of the men to come up from the trench. There were stains of vomit on his clothes and tears streaked the filth on his cheeks.

'They 'adn't any faces,' he whispered. 'No faces left.' He crossed the road to a squalid gin shop and we heard him bellow for spirits.

His tidings were repeated by the crowd and soon I heard mothers, they were mainly Irishwomen, keening for their dead. More men emerged and went directly to the gin shop. Pride and Passion, as she passed among the women, comforting and reviving them, appealed to Rimmer to intervene.

'Don't let them get drunk. There's no knowing what

51

they'll do in anger.'

'Come on,' said Rimmer, and led us to the shop. We were too late. The man who had come first from the trench was already intoxicated and was haranguing his comrades from the counter.

''Twas rats from the sewers as did it; you 'eard the poor little souls a-sayin' so. One o' them was my own little Rosie. Know what's left o' 'er? Bones and shreds o' skin. Raw flesh, like a carcase, 'angin' in the butcher's shop. Them damned rats steal our food an' foul our 'ouses. Now they're a-killin' of our children.'

'We won't get no 'elp from them loafers on the Board o' Works,' another continued, 'so I say we should 'elp ourselves. Go arter the devils an' slaughter 'em.'

Their words were approved with a roar and the men pushed past us, calling for more lights.

'Git 'em from Kimber's, git 'em from the candle factory,' cried a voice; and the mob ran towards a brightly-lit building farther along the road. Rimmer, Scud and I followed, while Durston, anticipating disorder, went with the constable to summon reinforcements.

Kimber's candle manufactory was the largest in London. Its wares illuminated the entire metropolis and in every major city masses were said, books were written and dinners consumed by the light of Kimber's gleaming tapers. The night shift had just begun. Pushing past an expostulating manager and bewildered workmen, the mob ran into the candle-room and milled around the moving belt of moulds into which tallow streamed from an automatic dispenser.

'Over 'ere!' came a cry and the men followed the belt across the room to a bank of pressurized blowers which expelled each cooled candle from its mould; there they began to grab at the rows of glossy sticks racked underneath. Armed with the thickest—'Bound for some Papist altar,' muttered Rimmer, disregarding Scud's religious sensibilities—the mob pushed its way back past the manager, who had barely recovered from its initial incursion, and streamed towards the trench. Shinning down the ropes and ladders that they had left there, the man rampaged at the

52

bottom, overturning barrows and piles of timber, seizing picks and axes, prodding and probing for an entrance to the sewer. We watched, helpless, from the edge. At length, one man, having wrenched off a hinged plate, gave a roar; we saw him beckon and point to an aperture; within seconds the mob had lit its candles and crawled in. Durston arrived with a squad of constables.

'We've failed,' said Rimmer. 'God knows what damage they'll do.'

'They're past caring,' muttered Scud. 'And if it had been mai little Bridie dead down theer, Ai'da done the same thing maiself.'

Durston spoke to the sergeant in command of the constables, who ordered his men down into the trench; but as the first of them touched the bottom, there was an explosion, the ground thrummed beneath our feet, and a flame roared from the aperture into which the mob had disappeared. The jet played briefly upon the boards and trestles around the trench before they ignited, and soon a mighty column of fire rose upwards, accompanied by thick skeins of smoke and an unmistakeable smell.

'Oh God!' moaned Scud. 'They've fired a gas main.'

We failed to discover how it had happened. Had a wavering candle ignited a leak from a hairline crack? Had a pick, driven through rotting brickwork, pierced the metal of a pipe? No one survived to tell us. The men in the sewer perished at once in the blast, and the policemen on the ladders were licked up and consumed in seconds.

The crowd of onlookers milled about aimlessly until we took charge. Rimmer organized a chain of women to pass buckets of water from the nearest pumps; Scud sent out squads of men to break up the frozen ground and stifle small subsidiary fires with shovelfuls of earth and snow; Durston and his police sergeant, having dispatched a warning to the gas company and summoned the parish fire engines, began to evacuate the mission and the nearby houses; while Pride and Passion enrolled me as a nursing orderly and set up a first-aid post for dressing burns inflicted by the blazing debris that had been showered upon the bystanders.

The fire spread to the gin shop. It had been among the first buildings to be evacuated, but the proprietor, his takings tripled by the mob's heavy drinking, had been loth to leave his money behind and had crept back. He must have been cramming his pockets when his wares ignited, for as the shop bloomed into flames, he appeared at the door, coat bulging, arms flailing, only to be sucked back into the vortex. He was not the only one to perish there: when the shop had been reduced to smouldering embers, another body was found at the back; a loitering thief, perhaps, or a vagrant draining empty bottles; man or woman, no one could tell, for the corpse had shrivelled to the size of a baby and disintegrated into ashes and flakes of charred bone when it was touched.

Once the gin shop was ablaze, we knew that Kimber's candle factory must be at risk. Durston himself went to advise the manager to evacuate it, but the fool refused, disdaining even to leave his desk in the candle-room or to invite Durston beyond the threshold. He had every confidence in the parish fire appliances, he shouted; they would soon arrive and have the fire under control. Durston remonstrated with him, his voice straining to carry over the din outside; this was no ordinary fire, he argued, but would grow in strength for as long as the gas fuelled it; it was imperative that the night shift be dismissed. The manager swelled: lose a whole night's production, certainly not! Never, admitted Durston later, had he come as near to committing assault and battery upon a fellow man, not even upon Lord Yelverton. But the argument had wasted essential time. A workman pointed to the tallow vats. In the growing heat their contents seethed like an alchemist's brew, while the moulded candles themselves were turning to liquid upon the factory floor. The manager bellowed again, but his words were lost as a tremor shook the building and flames sprang through the floorboards. Durston wasted no more time but called to the workmen to leave. They had valued their livelihood too much to leave their benches against the manager's orders; now, however, they saw that their very lives were in jeopardy and made for the door. The manager, trying to bar their way, was pushed to one side. He fell against the machinery of the conveyor belt and the tails of his coat were caught in its cogs. As he struggled to free himself, his hands became pinioned in the rollers and, whimpering pitifully, he was left ensnared as the flames fed greedily upon the oil and grease around him.

Meanwhile, the workmen had discovered the folly of their delay. When they tried to cross the smouldering floor to the door, they found it awash with scalding tallow which blistered the skin from their feet. Those behind, seeing the agony of their workmates as they dragged themselves to safety, made for a mezzanine floor that encircled the candle-room. They fought amongst themselves as they scrambled up the single wrought iron staircase that led to it, and several fell through the balustrade to lie threshing in the tallow beneath. Those who reached the top of the stair hammered at barred windows, trying to shift the iron that had rusted fast in its stone sockets, but in vain. The flames now reached the mezzanine, darting through the iron gratings from which it was formed and flickering over its wooden furnishings. The men found an unbarred skylight and, scaling a pile of the remaining furniture, clambered out on to the roof.

Durston could do no more to help them and turned to run back. But as he did so, he found that he, too, was in danger. A tide of tallow, the molten remains of hundreds of thousands of candles, washed over the threshold of the factory door and swirled towards him. Perceiving the threat not only to his own life but to those of the men who had crossed the burning floor and were now limping ahead of him, Durston began to yell like a maniac and ran among them, flinging them from the road. He had cleared it but for a single man, too blistered to do more than shuffle, when the tide grew in momentum. Durston seized the cripple and, with more strength than I would have thought he could muster, tossed him over his shoulder and began to run towards us. The swirling wax gained upon him, rivulets running ahead of him on which he slithered and slid and finally collapsed in a tangle of limbs. But just as the molten mass began to engulf him, women from the bucket chain drew abreast and dispersed it with repeated sluicings. Durston rose, resumed his casual mien and dabbed daintily at his brow.

'That damned waxing nearly brought about my waning,' he remarked, and turned to look, with us, at the factory.

The roof was now ablaze but men leapt in a stream through the flames, miraculously unharmed, save for the last two, whose passage we traced in the sky by the crest of fire from their hair to their waists.

'Poor devils,' said Durston and turned away.

'You did your best,' Rimmer consoled him.

'It wasn't good enough.' Durston was savage.

Twice that night I had seen him moved, and I had learned that despite his arrogance and languor, he was a brave man and sensitive. Indeed, I was coming to admire him as much as I admired Rimmer. Could he really be a liar? Had I made an absolute ass of myself? Was there not some totally rational explanation of the wretched business?

The parish fire-engines arrived, two ancient hand-pumpers that quaked on worm-eaten timbers. Their captains, one the sexton, the other a retired bo'sun, announced that they had sent for help to neighbouring parishes and to the metropolitan brigade. With luck, they added, Holborn Parish would send its recent acquisition, one of Merry-weather's patent steam fire-engines; the Holborn firemen had talked of nothing else since they had bought it and the men of St Giles wanted to see the marvel—indeed, they were more concerned with the prospect of assessing its performance than they were with tackling a blaze that was manifestly beyond their resources. They had not long to wait. A clanging bell and blaring hooter sounded high above the roaring flames and into view came the Holborn *Deluge*, swaying perilously behind four horses and manned precariously by six men. A vast steel boiler and copper tubes reflected the crimson glow from the sky and smoke streamed from a shining funnel. Its captain leapt from the iron chassis and brought his team into action. The hoses were unfurled and the steam valve thrown open; the pump exploded into action; and a thick jet of water shot 100 feet into the air before the range was corrected and it was driven deep into the sewer workings. Other appliances appeared: a ram-shackle contraption from Islington, two spanking new outfits from St Pancras and a French contrivance from Soho. Finally the metropolitan brigade arrived, and within four hours the fires were under control.

There remained the task of searching for the dead. Durston went into conference with the fire captains then led us aside.

'I took advantage of their obvious reluctance to send men into the sewer to suggest that we ourselves might carry out that part of the investigation. We are ignorant of what may be down there, and the fewer we let into our secret the better. Who would care to be first?'

Scud volunteered. Donning waterproof boots, he des-cended and, after poking gingerly about in the bottom of the trench, whistled us down. The sides and floor of the trench were still smoking but we trod warily and eventually found ourselves at the aperture through which the drunken men had entered the sewer. A sickening smell of burnt meat issued from it. Scud crawled in for a short distance then withdrew; for many yards ahead, he said, the floor was deep in roasted men and rats.

'Any war-lords?' asked Rimmer through a dampened rag.

'D'yees really want me tew faind out?' grinned Scud.

'Yes.' Rimmer was serious. If one had been, say, suffocated rather than roasted, McWhirrie might be keen to have the specimen for dissection. Anything we could learn of their anatomy and physiology would be of value.

Scud nodded, grimaced, and disappeared once more into the tunnel. He re-emerged fifteen minutes later to report that forty yards inside was a war-lord, wedged in a small branch sewer, in comparatively good condition.

Rimmer smiled his appreciation. 'Then it's a matter of simple logistics to extract him in secrecy and take him to a laboratory. Durston,' he addressed the civil servant, who was, I guessed, attempting to stop his thoughts from dwelling upon the contents of the sewer by bending them to the irreparable state of his topcoat, 'Durston, you're the administrator. Can you arrange it?'

57

Durston imagined that he could and returned to gloomy contemplation of his waxen broadcloth.

We climbed back up to the road and, midnight having long passed, decided to make for our beds. On the way we visited Pride and Passion in her mission, which had escaped with only superficial charring. She was busy playing Miss Nightingale to a dispensary full of invalids who were powerless to stop her ministrations. She paused as she swabbed a blistered arm and gave us her blessing for our deeds that night; to which Rimmer, embarrassed, rejoined that a cup of tea laced with whisky or rum would have been of more immediate value. We left her to grope for a retort and called for a cab.

Of these there were plenty. They had rolled up in relays for the past two hours, loaded with sightseers. One halted opposite me to disgorge its fare. I recognized the ponderous body at once: it was the man whom I had seen that afternoon—was it only ten hours ago? It seemed like a week—talking to Durston in the Cut. As I stared at him, I knew why the face was familiar: I had engraved it once as a rushed job, farmed out to my master's shop by the *Illustrated London News*. July, it had been—no, June. As soon as we were back in Little Newport Street, and Rimmer was regaling McWhirrie and Gunn with an account of our adventures, while Scud heated the poker to mull wine, I rummaged among Rimmer's bookshelves and eventually amassed a pile of *Illustrateds*. There he was: 10 June, three-quarter face and nicely cut too, though I thought it as shouldn't. Mr Anthony Norris. Warming my hands on the glass of spiced claret that Scud had handed me, I read the text that surrounded the picture:

> Mr Anthony Norris, who has been responsible in recent years for the construction of some of the most extensive estates of working class housing in the northern and eastern parts of the metropolis, this day addressed the Society for the Provision of Artisans' Dwellings. His speech was well received by an audience which included the Lord Mayor of London and the Duchess of Aston.

Obviously a gentleman of substance and good reputation, as Rimmer remarked when I told him what I had seen and showed him the magazine. Why should Durston deny that he had shared his company? The question nagged at me as I stumbled to bed over McWhirrie, Gunn, and Scud, who were roughing it on the floor.

The next day we awoke late to a sky of cumulus and a fresh fall of snow. We lunched off game pie and cheese and wondered how the rats would retaliate against the humans who had invaded their territory and burned and suffocated them. Gunn adhered to his theory that they would need food, and suggested that, following the animal warehouse stores, a hospital would make an easy target. Rimmer thought an attack upon a riverside grain warehouse was more likely. But neither of them knew how such assaults could be prevented or warning of them given, without arousing widespread alarm in the metropolis. McWhirrie listened as they theorized, a basket of scones from Gunn's aunt planted on his knee. When the debate lapsed, he brushed the crumbs from his whiskers and filled his pipe from Rimmer's tobacco jar.

'Ye're mebbe richt. But, masel', I gie the rats credit for mair foresicht. See, ye're aye thinkin' o' them as beasties. A gran' army, fairly that, but o' beasties. Noo me, I think o' them as men, an army o' men fechtin' an invader, an' I ask masel' the question: fit matters maist tae an army that's repellin' a furrin invasion? Rimmer, ye're the military mon, nae doot ye ken the answer?'

Rimmer—he liked the 'military mon'—considered. 'Mobility, I should say. An army in its own country has the advantage of shorter lines of communication than the enemy. But these have to be protected and kept clear so that forces can be moved swiftly wherever they are needed.'

McWhirrie imphed his approval. 'Noo, yon army below the grun', it has fine communications a'ready, in the sewers. But there's anither set, alongside the sewers, an' it has tae mak' siccer o' that yin afore the enemy can tak' it owre. Ye ken fit I mean?'

Rimmer looked baffled and Gunn was ensconced behind

The Times, as was his habit whenever McWhirrie held forth for anything longer than two sentences. But I had an inspiration.

'I know, sir,' I cried. 'The underground railway tunnels!'

McWhirrie imphed several times more in delight and offered me the last of the scones.

'Jist so. The tunnels o' the railways; and the maist important o' these, forebye, is—fit d'ye ca' it?'

'The Metropolitan Railway, of course!' Rimmer smote his brow. 'You think they'll overrun its underground lines?'

'If nae this time, then sin,' McWhirrie averred.

The professor, said Rimmer, should have gone to the Staff College. His talents were manifestly needed on the General Staff. It was Monday. Sunday had passed quietly. The rats had done nothing during daylight and we ourselves had been confined indoors by thick snow. But at night the enemy had moved into position and at dawn on Monday had attacked. By eleven o'clock Durston had joined us with a thick file of reports. McWhirrie, to Gunn's intense annoyance, had predicted the rats' objective precisely.

Durston's information was disjointed but gradually we assembled something like a chronological narrative. The first intimation of the offensive had been at King's Cross, where the Metropolitan Line shared a station with the Great Northern. A railway constable, checking the line for faults and discovering a loose bolt several yards along the western tunnel, had reached into a recess in the tunnel wall for some tools; teeth had clenched upon his hand and he had withdrawn it to find a rat dangling. He had shaken it off only to feel claws on his neck and back and the creatures' evil breath upon his face. He had run back to the platform, where another constable had helped him to break the animals' spines. But as they had stood there, resolving to complain to the station-master when he arrived, they had heard a raucous cry and a brown tide had debouched from the tunnel and had overrun the platforms. The two constables had taken to the stairs and on the ground floor of the station had locked themselves into a ticket booth. When the early shift of engineers had arrived at the station, they had seen two stricken faces peering through the window of the booth over a squirming brown carpet. The foreman of the shift had had the presence of mind to unhook a fire-hose and to force a path with it through the rats; he had extricated the constables mere seconds before the booth had been shattered by a thousand flailing tails. Slamming and bolting the exterior doors of the station, the shift had summoned the police, who, following their standing instructions, had reported the incident to Durston's office and had awaited his instructions. They had been warned not to re-enter the station but to erect notices explaining that it was closed temporarily, owing to a derailment in the tunnel. The shift had sworn secrecy upon pain of dismissal and departed. None of the city clerks who arrived two hours later to find the station shut guessed, as they grumbled, that inches from them swarmed a horde of snake-heads.

At the Paddington terminus there was no need to invent a derailment to explain the sudden closure of the station: two occurred there within five minutes. The first sign of the rats' presence had come when the driver of the earliest eastbound train, bringing her in gently from the sheds, had felt teeth entering his ear. Rigid with pain, he had let the engine accelerate, had blundered past a signal, and had felt the chassis rear up over the station platform before his legs had been crushed. Meanwhile, a second engine had been attached to the fixed boiler near the station, to be charged with steam enough to travel the length of the line. The engineer in charge had momentarily rested his hand upon the safety-valve of the boiler when a pair of rats had alighted upon his shoulders. As their teeth met in his cheek, his fingers had tightened, the valve had closed, and pressure in the boiler had soared to bursting-point. There had been an explosion; part of the boiler had smashed into the walls of the tunnel, bringing sections of brickwork down on the line; the frame and motion of the engine had become enmeshed with the rails; and the lagging and sheeting from the boiler, together with the feed-pipes and handrails, had flown in every direction to scythe down the line of men that came running at the sudden sound. The engineer himself had been blown thirty feet but survived to die of his infected bite.

But it had been at Baker Street station that the worst tragedy had occurred. A gang of platelayers had been sent deep into the tunnel there to repair a length of the eastward track to Portland Street. The men had just finished and had extinguished their lamps and packed their tools, when their foreman had become aware of pinheads of light in the tunnel walls. He had stretched towards one and had touched a snarling muzzle. The lights—unblinking eyes—had turned red and the rats had attacked. Meanwhile, above ground in the station, the departure of the first westbound train from Portland Street had been signalled by telegraph. The controller at Baker Street, assuming that the gang had by then cleared the line and left the tunnel, had acknowledged the message and had thus summoned twenty tons of wood and iron to bear down upon men who were struggling on the rails with wave after smothering wave of beasts. It had been the foreman who had heard the approaching engine first. Spreadeagled across the metal, beating at fifty sinuous bodies with a shovel, he had twisted his head to see the squat, bell-shaped engine emerge from the blackness. He had heard the screech of the driving-wheels as the engineer had thrown them into reverse, but they had locked and slid along the rails, shearing off his feet and decapitating the platelayer by his side. The train had arched above the track and rammed into the tunnel's sides, bringing the walls and roof down upon the men below. The foreman had watched with pain-glazed eyes as two slabs of stone had collided and wedged above his head, saving him from the rest of the tumbling debris, so that he had had time to gasp a report to his rescuers before he had died from shock and loss of blood.

Durston brought us up to date. All stations of the Metropolitan Line had now been closed. The directors of the company had been given an expurgated but nevertheless confidential account of the rats, and had agreed to put out a statement attributing the closure of the line to flooding from the Fleet River. It ran, encased in an iron pipe, beside part of the railway and leaks from it had in the past caused temporary stoppages in services. Fortunately, Durston ended, the rats had confined themselves to underground installations and had not entered the major termini or interfered with main-line trains.

'Nevertheless,' said Rimmer, 'they've cut us off from the one route, other than the sewers, by which we might have had a crack at them.'

Gunn, I noticed, looked thoughtful at these words but said nothing. It was not until later that I found out why.

Durston departed, and a gloom fell upon us as we digested his news and anticipated without enthusiasm Crashaw's ploy with his convicts. At length, McWhirrie put aside his pipe.

'Ach, it's as thick in here as a black hut at Hogmanay!' he declared. 'Come awa' oot wi' us tae Hammersmith. See fit Gunn and me's bin deein'.'

During the days and nights that Rimmer, Scud, and I had spent adventuring underground, McWhirrie and Gunn had done noble work on the surface. Although they had regularly attended us in Little Newport Street to hear reports of our meetings and our deeds, and to regale us with drink and victuals when we returned exhausted, their visits had come only at the end of meticulous toil; Gunn in the libraries and record-rooms of the metropolis, McWhirrie in Richard Owen's laboratories and in the reading-room of the Zoological Society. A report upon their researches was long overdue and the prospect of a trip into the rural west, along white-crusted roads, in crackling air, under filaments of cirrus, enticed us forth at once.

Gunn's aunt welcomed us with a table laden for tea. It was only after we had done justice to her bakings of bread, scones, and cakes and her bottlings of preserves and jellies that we adjourned to one of the two rooms which her lodgers had converted into studies. The room, which was immaculate, was Gunn's: papers sorted, piled, and weighted; books at attention, plans rolled and labelled. The floor was covered by a map of London. There was a mere nine-inch margin of board on which to circumnavigate it. Into the map were stuck pins, pins with coloured heads, by means of which Gunn had plotted every incident involving rats that he had discovered in his researches. We saw more clearly now, than at the Board of Works, how outrages were concentrated along the lines of the Middle Level and High Level sewer systems. But Gunn waited impatiently for us to notice something else: a blob in the middle of the map, where red pins (seventeenth century), blue pins (eighteenth century) and black pins (the present century) crowded so closely that they obscured the street-names entirely.

'It's a small, rectangular area,' said Gunn in response to Rimmer's enquiry, 'beginning at the riverside by Charing Cross, where Hungerford Market used to be until they demolished it a couple of years ago to build the station and the hotel, and running north towards Covent Garden. Inhabitants of this neighbourhood have suffered more from the depredations of rats in the last 250 years than those of any other part of London, the most squalid rookeries of the East End included. No matter which century, there has always been trouble with rats around Hungerford.'

He produced a sheaf of blue foolscap, closely written, and invited Rimmer to select a folio at random. Gratified at the result, which confirmed his assertion, he settled his glasses upon his nose and read:

Petition of the stallholders of Hungerford Market to the Mayor and Aldermen of Westminster, 7 May 1778. Whereas the stall-holders of the market at Hungerford have suffered greatly from the assaults of rats upon their persons and property (a declaration of which injuries and losses is appended hereto) and whereas the said stallholders, seeking redress of the said injuries and losses, have formed an association for the hunting and destroying of the said vermin, witnesseth this petition that the said stallholders request and desire that the said Mayor and Aldermen do furnish them implements and other articles necessary for the said purpose, for that it is to the common good of the city.

Gunn peered over his lenses. 'Just one of several attempts by the market tradesmen to put down the beasts. The council was able to help them but,' he fumbled for another folio, 'listen to the sequel. It is contained in a street ballad which I can confidently ascribe to the succeeding year.' And Gunn,

64

to my surprise and McWhirrie's unconcealed disgust, sang in a rounded baritone:

> Come all you bold tradesmen
> And list to the tale
> Of Thomas Tremain
> And his barrel of ale.
>
> He bought it and broached it
> And then did repair
> To treat all his friends
> At the Hungerford Fair.
>
> They came to his stall
> And drank bumpers so free,
> When up popped a rat,
> Saying, 'Give some to me.'
>
> They came to his stall
> And drank the barrel dry,
> When another rat came,
> Saying, 'Leave some for I.'
>
> But finding that Tom
> Had left nothing to quaff,
> The rats came in hundreds
> And carried him off.

'I trust,' McWhirrie growled, while Rimmer and I applauded to Gunn's evident delight, 'that we've exhaustit your repertoire. I'm nae here masel' for a musical soiree.'

'Evidence,' Gunn replied. 'It's prime evidence, my dear fellow. No matter how fanciful a street ballad may sound, it is inevitably founded upon fact. In my opinion, we have here a reference to some form of retaliatory attack by the rats, following the intervention of the stallholders' association.'

Rimmer nodded accord and asked Gunn what he knew of Hungerford and the market there. Gunn rifled through his notebooks: the site, he told us, had been occupied from

65

medieval times onwards by town houses of the nobility, and in the seventeenth century had contained the mansion of the Hungerford family. In 1669—he reached to his bookshelves and pulled down *Pepys* to read us the entry for 26 April—in 1669 the mansion had been burned down. Later Sir Edward Hungerford had received royal permission to hold a market in its place. There was nothing in the history of the site, Gunn concluded, to explain the frequency there of incidents involving rats; nevertheless, he was intensifying his search in that quarter.

McWhirrie now conducted us to his study. Unlike Gunn's, it was in utter disorder, a state not unanticipated, since McWhirrie's town clothes—rough tweed trousers, shabby black coat, tartan plaid and woollen bonnet—had prepared us for the worst. Every flat surface was littered with labelled shreds of bone, bitten scones, fragmentary notes, dissecting instruments, rough sketches, finished drawings, and dog-eared volumes. The floor, however, was mercifully clear save for a glass case containing a stuffed specimen.

'I've some guid news for ye a',' the professor announced. 'An' I'm nae needin' tae sing it tae ye forbye,' this with a malevolent look at Gunn, who snorted and stared with distaste at the partially-dissected limb which he had removed from the seat of his chair.

'Durston had yon deid war-laird fae the sewer workings at St Giles brocht tae the laboratory, an' me an' Owen spent a day takkin' it apairt. Man, it wis fairly the biggest rat I've ever seen, Owen tae, an' fit a time we had wi' it. Noo, there's twa things we fun'. *Primo*, its brain wis weel developit beyond that o' ony ornery rat. *Secundo*, it had a muscular capacity greater than any ither rodent. We wis fair stumpit by it. But then Owen thocht on Shaw's accoont o' the Malabar Rat. We went tae the buiks an' there wis oor answer. In size, strength, ferocity an' cunnin', oor war-lairds are gey like yon species fae the Indian coast. Onywye, file we wis talkin', alang comes an auld body fa kent weel the collections o' the museum; an' he tuk us ben tae a store-room faur they pit damaged specimens; an' he showed us this yin.' McWhirrie pointed to the massive, furred creature in the case

66

upon the floor. 'Yon big brute is a Malabar Rat, ancestor, as Owen and me believe, o' the war-lairds we're fechtin' the day.'

Gunn's aunt tapped at the door. A Rifleman stood behind her.

'Colonel Crashaw's compliments, gentlemen. He invites you to join him at Millbank Prison. The convicts are ready to depart.'

So the 'fechtin' was beginning again. Well, now, thanks to McWhirrie and Owen, we knew a little more about the enemy.

V
A second reverse

Darkness had fallen, bringing with it more snow, and it was a slow journey back to London. At last, however, our cabs stopped under mighty walls and I guessed that we had arrived at Millbank Prison. Warders met us at the studded door and asked us to identify ourselves, while more stared down at us from towers high above. I felt not unlike a Saracen of stunted growth, gaping up at a crusader's castle. Rimmer was also awed. When the guards, satisfied with his responses—I was still the indispensable amanuensis—swung open the door, he muttered, 'Hang it, even the creak of the hinges makes me feel like a felon.' We were escorted through an archway, into a yard, and along a narrow road between high walls with barred lights, to the centre of the octagonal complex. In front of us stood a circular house, the governor's residence, our guards told us, where the rest of our party had assembled.

Crashaw and two officers of the Rifles stood in the governor's study, talking to a fussy little fellow, whom we discovered to be the governor himself, and a lugubrious clergyman, who later introduced himself as the representative of the Prison Commissioners. Durston occupied a settle by the fire, with Scud, ill at ease, beside him. Crashaw nodded brusquely to us and continued his conversation, but Durston beckoned us over and proffered a file. Rimmer scanned it and pursed his lips. The rats, it reported, had taken their offensive in a new direction. Hitherto, their attacks had been confined to the north side of the Thames. Now, incidents were being reported from the south bank. Not on the scale to which we had grown accustomed, but of an extent sufficient to set editors of local newspapers from

Bermondsey to Lambeth sharpening their pencils and composing sardonic editorials on the 'vigilance' of the police and the 'efficiency' of the local authorities.

Bermondsey Market, the principal emporium for hides, had been the scene of the first outrage. A buyer, fondling a pile of new pelts, had seen them move independently under his hands, and had pulled one aside to reveal a dozen rats underneath, writhing and lashing their tails. Soon afterwards, at Barclay and Perkins, the largest metropolitan brewery, covering thirteen acres of prime land in Southwark, a maltman had hauled himself up into one of the lofts to find the mounds of malt there heaving and collapsing as a pack of rats burrowed into them. It had been the same in the brewery's twenty-three other lofts, save that in two, workmen had been buried and suffocated by the shifting grain. Meanwhile, a porter at the railway terminus of the London Necropolis Company in Lambeth had been stacking coffins for transportation to the company's cemetery at Woking when he had heard scufflings and had opened a lid. He had subsequently been unable to give a coherent account of his discovery, except that there had been rats . . . In each case the incursion had been brief; the rats had attacked swiftly and had withdrawn. But these, we guessed, were simply skirmishers. Somewhere behind them was the main column.

Crashaw finished his conversation with the governor and ahemmed for attention.

'We have a long night's work ahead of us, gentlemen,' he said, with his flair for the apposite cliché. 'Shall we make a start?'

The governor led us into a cobbled yard at the back of the house, where, under a guard of six armed warders, thirty men formed a circle, shivering in their prison drab, which was already saturated by the snow and clung to their rigid limbs. Hand-picked, they were, commented the governor, fit, keen, and, above all, reliable. Crashaw raised a sceptical eyebrow and inspected them, relishing the resentment that flickered for a moment at the level of his collar before dropping to his boots. The inspection over, he addressed

69

them. As I listened, I remembered his words to the Volunteers and wondered if he would achieve the same high standard of candour. He surpassed it.

'An unusual and diverting task awaits you,' he began and dragged back his lips in a smile. 'One that will enable you to perform a service for the population upon which you have hitherto preyed, and one that, if properly accomplished, will secure each of you remission of up to twelve months. Is that not so?' He turned to the governor, who nodded. 'There, you have the governor's word upon it.' He stopped, but there was no response. 'And what do you have to do for this?' he continued, lips tightening. 'A little rat-catching in the Covent Garden sewer. No more. If you do well, many of your,' he hesitated, seeking the right word, 'your comrades will be invited to serve in the same way. It is up to you to give such a humane scheme a first-rate start. Good luck to you.' That was all; nothing about the war-lords. If Crashaw had suspected a lack of resolution among the Volunteers, he had no doubt about its absence among the convicts.

His officers took charge, divided the men into groups of ten, assigned one guide and two guards to each, and ordered us into wagons that rumbled across the cobbles. Then, with Crashaw, they mounted and trotted off with our wagons lurching after them, the men in mine eyeing with envy my greatcoat and hat, while I responded with an uneasy grin and produced my sketch-book.

One sketch predominates. It is of Dicky Pitts, a hunched figure of seventeen with the seamed face of a man of forty; he chatted to me and picked my pocket. Lacking family and friends, he assumed that everyone was an enemy and treated all comers with the same amiable lack of loyalty, honesty, sentiment, and hypocrisy. A missionary in Whitechapel had taught him his letters; whereupon Dicky had deciphered a sign that said 'Books bought here', had stolen the mission library, and had lived for six months on the proceeds. He had become a mudlark, snapping up from the river-bed pieces of coal, iron, copper, and other oddments that dropped from barges, and selling them; eventually, he had decided to snap up the oddments before they dropped, and

70

had been caught rifling the barges' holds. Free again, he had graduated to 'stockbuzzing'—stealing handkerchiefs—dog-snatching and robbing drunks; with his profits, he had bought a suit, and a coat to cover his arm, and had 'worked the railways'—picking pockets on race trains—until his capture.

Pitts' adventures and the sketch-book shared my attention until our procession stopped on the line of the Covent Garden sewer. Rimmer descended with his party through a manhole at the southern end; my group was deposited at the now all-too-familiar King Street subway; while Scud disappeared with his group, to be deposited at the northern entrance. One of Crashaw's officers had dismounted and led us to a tarpaulin-covered mound on which a corporal and three Riflemen stood guard. Beneath the cover, we found protective clothing—Crashaw had learned one lesson, it seemed—cudgels and traps. The officer explained the details of the operation. In approximately fifteen minutes the sewer would be flushed; Bazalgette, I learned, had rounded up as many experienced flushermen as he could, and they had declared that, in their view, melting snow would reinforce the strength of the stream and the warrens would be effectively flooded. Once the flushing had finished and the water level in the sewer had fallen, we were to enter the sewer and move northwards and southwards, dislodging the remaining rats by hand and setting traps, until we should join up with our colleagues, when we were to depart. After some hours we should return to empty the traps and to disinfect the sewer.

We entered the subway, and immediately I was back in that novelette again, seized by the feeling of impending doom. In order to distract my mind, I returned aloft and requested permission from the officer, who had remained discreetly above ground, to go into the sewer and watch the flushing; Mr Rimmer, I added, had insisted that I should record as much of the operation as I could by sketching. The officer shrugged what I took to be assent and, while he remounted and rode off, I re-entered the subway and dropped through the manhole.

A party of flushermen was not far away and their obliging ganger explained what they were about. At the widest parts of the sewers were grooves; 'for the penstocks', Scud had told me when I had first noticed them, but I had not understood him. Now I discovered that wooden gates fitted into them—these were the penstocks. The 'lock-keeper' of the gang was busy adjusting their position as I watched, while the rest of the men were raking the deposit at the bottom of the sewer. The object was to dam the stream, when it was at its greatest, behind the penstock; and then, by releasing the gate, to let the accumulated tide rush through, scouring away the loosened deposit and sweeping away the rats. The lock-keeper straightened up from the penstock and nodded to the ganger, who reached into a recess in the sewer wall, drew out a hand-bell, and rang it. There came a multitude of diminishing echoes as our signal was relayed along the sewer. Silence fell. Suddenly the sound of bells returned. As it grew in volume, the ganger motioned his men into the wall recesses and, having sent the message onwards with his own bell, dragged me unceremoniously into a recess and on to a ledge two feet above the stream, so that our heads were bowed under the upper invert. A current of fetid air coursed through the sewer and set me retching. It preceded a torrent of water that swept round a bend in the course and rushed upon the penstock. The wooden board quivered in its grooves; water seethed at a level with its rim; but, just when it seemed that the eddies must pour over its lip, the board was released and the tide flowed through, swirling up our boots until it lapped at our knees. As its impetus slackened, the gang rushed out into the stream and began to rake the silt towards the middle of the channel, where the current flowed most fiercely, so that it was whirled away.

At length, I felt the stream suck its way slowly down my leg, and soon it flowed once more at its accustomed pace. The men mopped their faces, rested on their poles, and muttered amongst themselves that there had been a fair old heap to shift and that they could have done with twice their number. When they appealed to the ganger for confirmation, however, he ignored them; with a puzzled frown, he was sweeping his lantern along and around the sewer.

'Damnedest thing,' he murmured after some seconds. We waited. 'Nivver seen a single one o' them.'

When heroes in novelettes are not sensing impending doom, they are having sudden premonitions. I was having one now.

'No rats?' I asked.

'None,' he replied. 'Nivver flushed a sewer yet but I've seen 'em in 'undreds in the tide, drowned dead an' spinnin' along in the current. But this time . . .' He looked at the men. 'Anyone see anyfink?'

They shook their heads. The lock-keeper spoke up. 'Funny, now you mention it, but I nivver saw any afore the flushin' neither. Used ter be, they'd come at yer as soon as yer went near the penstock. But this time I nivver saw so much as a shadder.'

'Nivver 'eard nuffink meself,' said a third. 'Queer, if yer asks me.'

Not really, I thought. Was it likely, after all, that the beasts to whom McWhirrie had attributed almost human intelligence, would let themselves be drowned so easily? Once again we had underestimated them. I excused myself and climbed to the main floor of the subway, where guards and convicts alike regarded me without interest. Only Dicky Pitts had a greeting.

'Flushin' over then? Ken we go down?'

I did not know what to answer. If our experience had been repeated elsewhere in the sewer, then clearly the flushing had not had the effect that Scud had looked for; in which case, the prisoners were advancing, with nothing save cudgels to defend themselves, against an enemy that had already put armed Volunteers to flight. Yet Crashaw had given his orders. Had I the right to contravene them? It was a dilemma that Samuel Smiles, say, or Mr Kingsley could have solved without hesitation. It would have presented no problems to the Duke of Wellington and certainly none to Mr Ruskin. But it was altogether too much for a sixteen year-old amanuensis, no matter how indispensable; so I temporized.

'Better give the flushermen time to get out,' I said and sat down next to Pitts.

A quarter of an hour passed. The gang emerged, tired and morose now, and departed. I had still not solved my dilemma.

'Ready then?' asked Pitts; and, without waiting for my reply, he swung himself into the manhole.

As I saw his impudent grin, and thought of Bunce, Sweetlove, Winser, Gotto, and Gilshinan, and of the children who had died in the omnibus and the men who had perished in the fire, I arrived at my decision.

'Stop, Dicky!' I shouted. 'There's something you ought to hear first.'

The convicts, however, had no intention of listening; for as I opened my mouth to say 'Danger', someone clouted me hard behind the ear, and the word came out as a billowing cloud that smothered me in blackness.

I awoke to find Rimmer's eyepatch an inch from my nose. This did not surprise me, since I had been dreaming of Little Newport Street, and had fancied that we had been sitting round the fire, burning our mouths on baked potatoes. Gradually, the pain in my mouth, a bitten tongue, spread to my ear and to my head, and I groaned.

'Not,' remarked Rimmer, 'an affectionate greeting for old friends. You're an ungrateful devil, Matt.'

'When he sees what he's wakened tew,' commented Scud, who sat nearby, 'he'll groan even louder.'

I looked around me. We were in a vaulted chamber, almost every foot of which was occupied by racks of barrels and bottles. In the centre was a boiler, pipes from which traversed every wall.

'Clapperton's wine-stores,' said Rimmer. 'Best stock in town. Kept at a perfect temperature. Wish I could afford to buy my port here.'

The prisoners congregated on the other side of the chamber. They had broached several casks and were already staggering. There was a trickle at my neck, blood, I imagined; it was only when I tried to staunch it, that I found that my hands were tied, my feet as well. Rimmer chuckled, and I saw that he and Scud were both trussed too. Dicky Pitts left his group and came towards us.

'He's a friend,' I muttered to Rimmer. 'He'll help.'

'Feelin' better?' asked Dicky. When I nodded, his grin widened and he drove his boot into my ribs. 'Then see ye lie there an' say nuffink,' he snarled and returned to the convicts.

'If he's one of your friends,' drawled Rimmer, 'I should hate to meet your enemies.' Smarting from the blow and humiliation, I made no reply. 'And if you think it's all an act to conceal his good intentions,' Rimmer continued, 'dismiss the notion. As far as Scud and I can discover, he's one of the ringleaders.'

Scud told me what had happened. It was apparent that some sort of escape attempt had been in the convicts' minds from the moment that they had been chosen for special duties. It had been simply a matter of adapting their plan to suit whatever were the circumstances in which they found themselves. We had all been overpowered in the same way; Scud and Rimmer, having thicker skulls than I, had suffered less; the guards had fared much worse. Scud indicated a row of bodies along one side of the wine-store, whose contorted limbs showed that they had resisted and had died violently. The prisoners had regathered and had advanced further into the sewer; one of them, scrambling into a large gully, had discovered an aperture that led to Clapperton's premises and they had spent the past thirty minutes there, arguing over their best route of escape and sampling the wine-merchants' wares.

'They're fallin' out among themselves already,' ended Scud. 'See, theer's some o' them wants tew leave the way they come an' trai their luck with the sojers, an' theer's others want to go farther down the sewer and faind a manhole that's not guarded.'

Rimmer gave an embarrassed hrm. 'There's something I should, perhaps, add,' he said. 'They've kept us alive hitherto, in case they need us again as guides. But a certain guarded something in their manner, demonstrated by your friend, suggests that they don't intend to let us accompany

75

them to the surface. They might cut our throats, as they cut the guards', or they might leave us fettered in the sewer. Knowing what we do about the rats, I'm not sure that a slit throat wouldn't be preferable.' He hesitated. 'Not depressing you, am I?'

Before I could muster enough irony to assure him that I found his words wildly uplifting, the convicts reached a decision and Pitts sauntered over to us again.

'We're restin' 'ere fer a while,' he explained. 'Ken't let all this liquor go to waste now, ken we? Afraid my mates don't fency yer company, so just bide quiet. We'll deal with yer proper afore we go.' His eyes wandered to the dead guards, leaving us little doubt as to the manner in which we would be dealt with. He turned to me. 'Enjoyed our little chat, I did. Tell y'what. I'll take yer 'andsome topcoat as a memento of a charmin' hencounter.'

This he did, unfastening my hands momentarily while he jerked my arms out of my coat sleeves; then he swaggered off to join the convicts, who were broaching fresh casks, letting the wine flow in wavering streams across the uneven flags of the floor. Which goes to prove that Rimmer had, at times anyway, no eye for the complexities of a man's character. For in the few seconds that he had fiddled with my hands, Dicky Pitts had loosened my bonds in such a way that, as soon as the convicts were deep once more in their potations with their backs to us, my hands were free and I was surreptitiously chafing my wrists.

I waited for about twenty minutes. The convicts were guzzling the wine and spirits wantonly now, splashing their faces with costly madeira and spraying each other with champagne. Dicky Pitts, I observed, drank little, although he made a pretence of gulping from a flagon on his arm. I was not, therefore, surprised when, the convicts having discovered a large stock of brandy, he detached himself unobtrusively from the throng and edged from cask to cask towards the gully. He slid into it and, catching my eye before he finally disappeared, winked, and flashed his grin; then vanished. I kicked Rimmer's ankle and nudged Scud, showing them my free hands. They wriggled close and I untied them. The carousal in the store became wilder; the prisoners danced with one another and indulged in drunken horseplay. Following the route behind the casks that Pitts had taken, we made for the gully, slithered down it, and set off in what we imagined to be the direction of the King Street subway.

'What are we going tew dew about thim convicts, sor?' asked Scud.

'We'll have to report their escape,' Rimmer replied. 'After all, they killed six guards and were going to do for us as well. But, hang it all, Crashaw as good as sent them to their deaths. I'm not sure that he isn't as much a criminal as they are. We'll say nothing of young Pitts' departure in advance. Least we can do, what?'

I was glad that Dicky had escaped, and hoped that by now he was somewhere safe above ground. This hope became a fervid prayer when the drunken shouts of the convicts, which still echoed behind us in the sewer, were interrupted by a raucous cry, a cry that I dreaded beyond all other, the cry of a war-lord. I turned to go back to the wine-store but Rimmer spun me around.

'There's nothing you can do,' he declared. 'Even if we could make them understand their danger, they are too far gone in drink to save themselves.'

I hesitated. But even as I did so, the drunken shouts became screams, became shrieks of pain and terror. We ran onwards to the subway, splashing through the stream until we reached a section of the sewer that I was coming to know well, and stopped under the manhole to the surface. None of us felt proud of our flight. Samuel Smiles, Mr Kingsley, the Duke of Wellington, and Mr Ruskin would all, doubtless, have displayed more resolution, but we were merely two frightened men and a boy, a boy who awoke for many nights afterwards with the screams of the convicts vibrating in his ears.

We reported to Crashaw in St Paul's Church and warned him that the number of survivors might be small.

'They were dispensable,' he remarked. 'Next time we must send more guards.'

I expected an outburst from Rimmer but none came. Instead, he nodded. 'You'll inform the Prison Commissioners, of course?' he commented.

'Of course,' replied Crashaw.

'They'll want to know the precise details of the way in which the guards and prisoners died,' Rimmer continued.

'Naturally.' Crashaw was puzzled. 'But I have your report.'

'Not good enough,' Rimmer told him. 'Great sticklers for protocol, these fellows. You'll have to go down and verify our statements.'

'I see no reason . . .' Crashaw began.

'Afraid?' asked Rimmer.

In reply, Crashaw picked up his gloves and, calling for an officer to accompany him, left the vestry. We waited. Ninety minutes later, he returned. There was a smell of brandy about him, which I thought must have come from the debris in the wine-store, but then I saw him take a flask from his pocket and pull hard on it. He groped for his chair, sat heavily, and held his head.

'Satisfied?' demanded Rimmer. 'You have nearly sixty deaths to your credit. Now you have seen what manner of deaths they were.'

We left Crashaw sitting at the vestry table, brandy flask before him, and returned to Little Newport Street; Scud joining us for another hard night upon the floor. As Rimmer fumbled with his latchkey, I felt a touch upon my arm. Propped against the wall beside me was my topcoat, and inside it was Dicky Pitts.

'Where did . . .' I began.

He forestalled the question. 'Bin follerin' yer, ain't I?' he grinned. 'Reckoned as 'ow one good turn oughter be repaid. Vittals, I want, an' a new rig an' some shekels. 'Ow 'bout it?'

We invited him in, fed him, and thanked him for his help in our escape. As he wolfed cold pie and pickles, he noticed the *Illustrated London News* in which I had found the picture of Anthony Norris. It still lay open at the page and Dicky, hauling it on to his knee, examined the illustration closely.

'Good likeness, that,' he said. 'Looks better 'ere than 'ee do in real life.'

'Norris?' I asked.

Dicky shook his head. 'Dalton. Tommy Dalton. That uster be 'is nime. Thin as a pole, 'ee were then, I've 'eard. Now 'ee's Enthony Norris, wiv chins 'enging down to 'is watch-chain. Got on in the world, 'ee 'as.'

'You know something of him?' questioned Rimmer.

'I should say so,' Dicky chuckled and, filling his mouth with cheese and what was left of a loaf, told us, a trifle indistinctly, what he knew.

Tommy Dalton had begun his career on the river-bed, like Dicky, but twenty years earlier. Nevertheless, when Dicky went to work, Dalton's name was still remembered around Wapping and Shadwell for the vigour and unscrupulousness with which he had pursued his trade. He had graduated from mudlarking to dredging—coming out early to scoop up the coals that had been spilled in transmission from barges to wharf. He had rapidly increased his profits by helping himself to bags of coal from the barges themselves, covering their contents with mud and passing them off as dredged coal. He had also built up a connexion with the ships' chandlers along the waterfront; and at the same time as he had relieved the barges of their coal, he had snapped up brass and copper fittings from schooners alongside and had sold them to the chandlers at prices which threw legitimate instrument-makers into despair. His next step evoked Dicky's highest admiration. Having won the trust of the chandlers, Dalton had proceeded to extort money from them, threatening to expose them as receivers of stolen goods. When they had responded by sending a gang of lightermen after him, he had recruited his own force of mudlarks and dredgers and had routed his opponents. For several years afterwards, he had forced the chandlers, and indeed most of the other waterfront shopkeepers, to pay money to him regularly for protection against theft or arson; and he had indulged in both, occasionally, to lend cogency to his demands.

'Why,' said Dicky, 'I've 'eard as 'ow one time there was

nigh on two 'undred coves, in one line or anuvver, a-payin' him fer the right to trade.'

Dalton, however, had tired of the limited view from his Wapping den and of the still more limited company with which he shared it. He had sold his organization to the owner of a school of pickpockets, three brothels, and a coiner's, who wanted to diversify still further. And, having pocketed the extravagant price that he had demanded, and having evaded the ambush by which the purchaser had hoped to recover it, he had disappeared for six months. When he had reappeared, his gaunt cheeks had plumped out, his clothes concealed with grace the beginnings of a belly, and he had introduced himself on the Stock Exchange and in Kensington drawing-rooms as Anthony Norris. He had invested his money in land; not fashionable tracts in the West End, but small patches of sour grass near the railways in North London. As the railway companies had expanded and required additional land for sidings and shunting yards, he had sold off his patches for large sums and had bought more; larger stretches this time, undrained and unkempt. As the demand for houses near the railways and the expanding industrial areas of London had grown, he had built upon his sites, sweating the cheapest labour he could find, and quelling any opposition to his methods through a team of brutal overseers who knew nothing of building but were skilled with the knife and the bludgeon. Norris's houses lacked style and charm—if you look at Doré's *London*, you will see several examples of his contribution to the city's architectural heritage—but they were eagerly acquired by Jewish and Irish immigrants, who let them at extortionate rates to less fortunate compatriots. There had been complaints about Norris's shoddy workmanship and his business practices; but, in addition to land, Norris had spent his money on politicians in Westminster and on the Board of Works, who widely represented his building enterprises as generous contributions towards the housing of the working classes. His name was at the top of subscription lists for new churches and ragged schools, and two streets, a terrace, and a crescent had been named after him.

80

'I've 'eard it said,' added Dicky, 'as there's talk of 'im bein' Sir Enthony Norris soon. Fect is, 'ee might even end up as Saint Enthony Norris, way 'is luck 'olds.'

Dicky's gossip petered out. That it was more than idle hearsay, however, we proved by seeking confirmation from Bazalgette—'Whenever I hear of some poor family dying in squalor in one of his hutches, I swear I'd like to take him by his greasy jowl and throttle him'—and from a journalist friend of Rimmer—'Old George Hudson and Anthony Norris are the two greatest villains of the age; but whereas King George lost his crown, Anthony's fly enough to stay on top until he dies.' When Dicky had departed, wearing a quantity of clothes (which we had given him), and carrying a large number of rings, razors, brushes and books (which we had not), Rimmer shook his head.

'Six weeks surveying life along the river, Matt,' he said, 'and it's only now that we learn of the career of Mr Dalton-Norris. We're green, that's what, green.'

Scud commiserated. 'Thought Ai knew a bit about the river folk tew, but Ai nivver heard tell of the laike o' Norris before.'

Another late night. Three o'clock, I think it was, before we stretched out on our beds, with Scud curled up in front of the fire. It seemed that I had barely drawn my first deep breath when there was a fearful din at the door. I peered at the clock and found that it was almost noon, although the ragged mass of fractostratus above made it seem like dusk. McWhirrie and Gunn were on the doorstep, McWhirrie in a state of high excitement, while Gunn beamed and executed waltz steps. They bustled in and insisted upon an immediate lunch; then, when Rimmer had heated chocolate and I had toasted sausages, the professor divulged their news.

'We ken . . .' he said.

'That is,' said Gunn, 'we have good reason to believe . . .'

'Wheesht! We ken fine noo a' aboot oor rats an' oor war-lairds.'

'We have, at least, formulated a theory which is sustained in every particular by reliable data . . .'

'Man, wull ye haud yer bletherin' tongue. We ken fine

81

faur they cam' fae an' hoo it happenit.'

Having thus engaged our curiosity, they clamped their mouths fast upon their sausages and would say no more than that we must repair with them directly to the British Museum. Gunn was nevertheless so excited that he snatched Rimmer's second mug of chocolate from him and tossed it into the sink; while McWhirrie achieved the unusual feat—for him—of leaving food uneaten on his plate, although he thought better of his rashness before we left and returned to stuff it partly in his mouth and partly in his pockets for later.

Within twenty minutes we were passing under the front colonnade of the museum, through the entrance hall, and down the long, narrow passage that led to the reading-room of the library. Under its gilded dome, in the gloom that was barely dispelled by the candles at each table, we were met by the top-hatted superintendant, who led us to a small room beyond, in which an attendant stood rigidly to attention at a desk on which lay a single printed leaf and a calf-bound volume.

'I understand, gentlemen,' said the superintendent, 'that some conversation may in your case be necessary. I have, therefore, had your items placed here temporarily and have asked Beevers to wait upon you.'

'This,' said Gunn, as the superintendent withdrew amidst murmurs of appreciation, 'is Beevers, blessed among men now and forever, amen; the unraveller of our mystery, namely, how did a species of London sewer rat come to acquire the characteristics of the Malabar variety? Beevers, would you like to explain or shall . . .'

'Oh, if you would, sir,' said the attendant. 'I'm sure it's not my place to . . .'

'Gladly,' Gunn continued, evidently gratified at the opportunity to expound, and, perching his plump posterior upon the desk, began. Beevers, he explained, had been fetching books for him since the beginning of his quest; astonished first of all at their quantity and then at their diversity, he had one day asked Gunn the subject of his researches.

82

'Not a liberty I am accustomed to take with our gentlemen,' interpolated the attendant, 'but me curiosity got the better of me.'

Learning that Gunn's enquiries pertained to rats, the attendant had brightened, for he had bred rats as a boy and had not forgotten his interest in the subject. He had followed the historical bent of Gunn's studies and, emboldening himself again two days previously, had offered to show Gunn something of interest. Gunn, filling foolscap with a mass of facts that enabled him to stick more pins in his map but that brought him no nearer an explanation of the nature of the war-lords, had been glad to lay aside his pencil. He had tolerantly awaited the attendant's reappearance with what he imagined would be a quaint engraving or a newspaper cutting with which he was already familiar. To his surprise, however, Beevers had returned with a Restoration handbill, one that Gunn had never before heard of, nor seen catalogued in any bibliography.

''Cos why? 'Cos it had only just this week turned up in a bundle of manuscripts another gentleman has been consulting,' explained the attendant. 'And Mr Love, as was fetching for him, passed it to me to give to the superintendant; but seeing as how it mentioned a rat, I kept it to one side for to take a closer look at it.'

A good thing for us that he had, resumed Gunn, otherwise it would have disappeared from sight again for years amid all the uncatalogued ephemera.

'This is it.' Gunn picked up from the table the quarto sheet; it was badly printed, with irregular spacing, broken type and smeared ink. We huddled round his shoulders while he declaimed its contents aloud—never one to miss the theatrical element in an occasion, was Gunn.

BRAVE NEWS FROM HUNGERFORD

Strange and Diverting Exhibition

It is reported that many in the Town do frequently resort now to the new Market in Hungerford House. The reason whereof is the arrival and exposition there, by Capt. Humphrey Crispe of the *Leonora*, new from the Coromandel Coast, of a Monstrous Rat.

This Beast, a Giant of its Species, doth with skill disport itself for the Entertainment of the Multitude. It will walk and run to command, and can, at the Captain's Behest, roll Balls into Cups, take Food from but one Platter midst many, and perform a Dance of Grace and Intricacy upon its Hinder Legs. Being not only greater in its Proportions than any known of its kind, and also of Intellect advanced beyond all other, Capt. Crispe hath dubbed it *Rattus Rex*, that signifieth The Rat King, and hath wrought for it a Crown for its head and Royal Garments for its Limbs. This Wonder is exhibited Daily next the stall of William Crispe, that bears a rich Array of Yarns and Linen.

'Is the handbill dated?' asked Rimmer.

'No,' replied Gunn, 'but it contains a clue. The *Leonora* was undoubtedly a vessel of the East India Company. Now, I am fortunate in having among my relatives a former clerk of the company, and he arranged that I should consult its registers. Humphrey Crispe made only one voyage with the *Leonora*; he put into London on 25 September 1690.'

'Interesting,' said Rimmer. 'But how is it connected with our war-lords?'

'By this announcement in *Mercurius Aureus*, a government broadsheet of November the same year,' replied Gunn and began to declaim once more.

Friends of France lurk in our midst: they creep along the ground, these canting snakes; they crouch beneath stones, these Jesuitical toads; they hide in the sewers, these Romish rats. And like the King Rat of Coromandel that flaunted itself before the populace at Hungerford Fair, yet is now escaped and roams none knoweth where, so are they, once much vaunted, now hiding deep in foul blackness.

'We believe,' McWhirrie had assumed the role of expositor, 'that a Malabar rat fae the east coast o' India—that's Coromandel, ye ken—was capturit an' trainit be yon Crispe, exhibitit at the mercat, escapit, an' foon' its wye doon intae the sewers.'

'There,' Gunn wanted a share of the summation, 'it bred with the existing population and passed on its intelligence and size to that strain we now call the war-lords.'

'An' they,' McWhirrie took over once more, 'syne cam'

tae dominate the ithers, an' owre mony years spiet upon the folk aroon' an' learnit somethin' o' their wyes. Noo, we ken that rats hae aye takken it ill fan fowk hae meddlit wi' the sewers. Weel, wi' the war-lairds tae lead them, their attacks grew stranger. But fan wurk began on Bazalgette's drainage scheme, they must hae thocht their hale wurld wis fa'in' in aboot their heids. An' then on tap o' a' that, there wis the earthquake; it doubled their fear an' made them a' the mair ferocious.'

'And why were so many incidents concentrated upon the area around Hungerford Market?' Gunn waved his spectacles in the direction of Charing Cross. 'Because that is where Rattus Rex must first have fled; that is where he bred; and that is where his successors became concentrated. And that, we believe, is where the seat of power still lies. Somewhere, not a mile from us, is the point from which the rats that terrorize London are commanded.'

'Then that,' declared Rimmer, 'is where we must strike next.'

VI
The home front

The rats forestalled us. The pack that had attacked the convicts in Clapperton's wine-store did not return to the sewers but wandered abroad; so much, at least, we deduced later. By the time that we had departed from the British Museum, congratulating ourselves on the discovery of the origins of the war-lords, they had moved from the vintner's into a nearby theatre, the York, where they remained unnoticed until evening, midway through the first act of the pantomime *Harlequin Made King*—'a feast of fun and frolic'. When Columbine—'Miss Harriet Vokes, sprightly songstress'—retired to the green-room to lubricate her vocal chords with a little gin-and-water, she found herself surrounded by them. Hitting in one scream a note to which she had never before aspired, she fled in terror, upsetting a candlestick. It was while she stood shaking in the wings, trying to explain the cause of her fright to the stage manager, that smoke from the heap of costumes upon which the candle had fallen began to spiral through the planks of the stage. It was noticed by Pantaloon—'the great little Ravallo'—who was wrestling at the time with a giant trombone and a bucket of water—'moments of immeasurable merriment for all the family'. Showing considerable resource, he emptied his pail over the spot and improvised an exit. A minute later the curtain came down and Ravallo returned to peer through it—'as droll in his face as his figure'—and beg the audience to disperse calmly. A drunken man, ten women and twelve children—'a spectacle to hold hundreds in awe'—obeyed him without undue reluctance and, crossing the road, awaited with greater enthusiasm than they had displayed throughout the performance, the arrival of the fire-engines.

But by the time that the engines had brought their hoses into play, there was little left of the York's interior; wings and flats of wood and canvas, domes and balustrades of lathe and plaster, were soon transformed into a silt of ashes and water whence projected charred beams and twisted girders.

When a report of the fire and its cause reached Durston, he dispatched a note to us and we met him on the blackened site. He greeted us with the reflection that, while the rats had displayed unexpected taste and discrimination in closing that particular show, he hoped that they would not habitually take their criticism to such extreme lengths; a letter to the manager would normally suffice. His flippancy masked his anxiety. It was no longer possible, he admitted, to play down outrages of this sort. Enquiries, both personal and written, were arriving at the Home Department by the hundred; the London papers were combining their accounts of incidents with an increasing amount of speculative comment; and, a consummation devoutly to be dreaded, hints had been received that a question was to be asked in the House. His office, he said, had taken immediate action to prevent any further disturbance of the rats. From his pocket he pulled a sheaf of printed leaflets: they were circulars on Home Department stationery, addressed to all manner of contractors, builders, and plumbers, ordering work underground or in the vicinity of sewers to cease. Another batch contained notices to be posted at subways, manholes, and other entrances to the sewers, forbidding unauthorized access upon payment of heavy fines. The reason for the prohibitions was given in the vaguest terms: 'to avoid undue disturbances of essential subterranean works'; 'in order to prevent interruption of major sanitary undertakings'; 'with a view to expediting certain work underground essential to the health and security of the metropolis'; and so on.

'I do not for one minute imagine,' said Durston, 'that the percipient population of London will be fooled. People seem aware that some sort of trouble has been encountered in the sewers, though not, thank goodness, of its extent and gravity.'

'Now there, sor, ye may be wrong.' Scud had joined us,

sent on from Little Newport Street, as he explained, by Gunn and McWhirrie. He handed a crumpled handbill to Durston. 'It was given me bai a friend. Ai'll not name him, so don't ye go askin' me.'

Durston read it aloud.

To all working men and friends of the working man. In every parish of the metropolis DEATH now lurks. Where once the CHOLERA stalked stealthily in silence, there now flits a new foe, not one dash less deadly. THE RAT. Know thy enemy. He is big and brown with a lashing tail and teeth tipped with poison. He hides in your house and he strikes where he will. Why? Because he has friends who aid and abet him. Who are they? They are to be found in the House of Lords and the House of Commons, on the Board of Works and in every vestry office. They are the complacent, conceited, conservative politicians, who eat while we starve, drink while we suffer; make merry while beasts bite our babies and bear them away. They are RATS of another species . . .

He returned the paper to Scud.

'Not much of a stylist, your author; overdoes the alliteration, rather; and he really should find a decent printer. But I take your point. He knows the nature of the problem and is making political capital out of it.'

As we walked back to Soho together, Rimmer, who had been uncommonly subdued, stopped by the entry to a close.

'Look there,' he said. 'D'ye see anything strange?'

We peered into the courtyard. Washing flapped in the wind. Dirty water streamed down its gutters. A dog sat and scratched.

'Nothing,' said Durston. 'It seems quite unexceptionally dismal.'

But I knew what Rimmer meant, for the same thing had occurred more than once to me in the past few days, as we had gone about the town. Unlike Durston, however, I had graduated from Pratt the engraver's window well versed in every detail of rookery life.

'There are no children playing,' I explained. 'Each court that we've passed has been deserted.'

'Exactly,' said Rimmer.

Just then, an infant scuttled from a doorway and squatted beside the gutter. Its mother pursued it.

'Come aht o' that, ye brat,' she scolded, 'afore the rats can get ye.'

'I rest,' said Rimmer, 'my case.'

Durston nodded.

'I told Miss Tiptree once,' Rimmer continued, 'that if we proclaimed the danger of the rats, the public would lose its senses. Despite our precautions, I think that time may soon be upon us.'

Durston summoned a hansom. 'I'll inform Yelverton,' he said. 'He has a way with the press. Perhaps we can soothe the public breast for a little longer.'

We saw the first results of Yelverton's efforts on the following day; Christmas Eve, I realized with a start. Three principal newspapers carried editorials which referred in casual terms to recent public disquiet over matters concerning health and hygiene; they took the liberty of informing their readers that these were but minor matters involving the rodent population of the sewers—'nothing more than has troubled the metropolis regularly in the past and will doubtless do so regularly in the future'; they assured their subscribers that London boasted a sewer system that was the envy of Europe; and they emphasized that the health and security of the populace were the subject of constant vigilance by the Board of Works. We bought a selection of local newspapers and found that Yelverton had deployed his influence there, too. Editors from both sides of the river, who had recently sniped at the Board of Works and its officials, now asserted that this had been no more than playful encouragement, in no way to be construed as criticism of the strenuous efforts which the guardians of the metropolis at all times made to protect London from hazards to health and welfare. A note from Durston later in the day informed us that Yelverton had held secret meetings with the editors and proprietors of every daily and weekly newspaper in London and had received a promise from them to reduce to a minimum all discussion of episodes involving rats for a period of seven days. 'That,' the note ended, 'gives us a breathing-space. His lordship has his uses!'

Editors and proprietors might promise what they pleased, but they could not pledge all the journalists of London, particularly those whose speciality was the exposure of secrets, men like Joseph Xavier Maginn and Saintly Hodges. They were Americans, fathered respectively by an Irish immigrant and a lapsed Mormon, who endowed their sons with a sketchy education and a thirst for hard liquor. Unable to make the former provide for the latter, the two boys became partners in the Hallelujah Mine, west of Carson City (where they lost their stake); deckhands on a clipper out of San Francisco (where they lost their breakfast); and proprietors of a gaming-house in New Orleans (where they lost their shirts). They decided that their fortune lay in New York and their decision, for once, was right. They had, they discovered, a talent for sensational journalism and could, said Rimmer, from whom I had their biographies, attend a Christian Ladies' Sewing Circle, expose it in 200 words as a cover for unbridled lust and corruption, call for a meeting of protest, and see the departure of a posse of civic-minded vigilantes to ride the ladies out of town on a piece of four-by-two, all in the space of a day or, if they made the early editions, an afternoon.

It had been in New York, at the outbreak of the Civil War, that Rimmer had met them. Convinced that he was a British agent, intriguing in the northern camp, they had, in a series of pungent articles for the *Clarion*, induced a dozen politicians to demand his deportation. Rimmer had sought them out, taken them to a saloon, and (inflicting permanent damage, he averred, upon his liver) had outdrunk them in whatever liquor they had chosen. That had been enough to assure them that he was an honest man. Eighteen hours later, surrounded by an admiring throng and balancing perilously upon a mound of empty, rolling bottles, they had improvised in effusive amity a measure compounded from the Americans' memories of ancestral jigs and Rimmer's blurred recollections of the eightsome reel, and had tripped it to the tune of 'Yankee Doodle'.

Maginn and Hodges had then come to London, staked by

the *Clarion* to luxurious hotels and unlimited liquor, while they sent off a series of newsletters from Europe's capitals, slanted to provide a war-weary America with the reassurance she needed, that the supercilious cities across the Atlantic were no more than dismal conglomerations of filth and squalor, masked by tinsel splendour. Ten days before we had learned of the menace of the rats, they had visited Rimmer. We had ended an insouciant evening rolling drunk in charge of three police truncheons, a mechanical chimney-sweeper, a large plaster statue of the Prince Consort, and a coalman's horse and cart, and dogged by a crowd which was under the impression that Maginn intended to cross the Thames on a tightrope, an impression that Maginn himself shared until we forcefully disabused him of it. When last we had seen them—Maginn all elbows, knees, and feet, with a jaw like an anvil; Hodges with an ursine torso, a leonine head, and a vulpine expression—they had been driving the coal-cart around Trafalgar Square, convinced that they were charioteers in a Roman circus.

We heard no more of them until the day after Yelverton's meeting with the press—Christmas Day (distinguished in Rimmer's establishment only by his excessive liberality with the brandy after lunch). Durston called us to his office and there we found Maginn swigging whisky, shocked but outwardly defiant. Durston was severe.

'This gentleman,' he said, 'appears to have contravened every single order that the Home Department has issued on the subject of rats, and has accomplished the very thing that we hoped to avoid—a fresh disturbance in the sewers.' He addressed himself to Maginn. 'Perhaps you would care to repeat your account. Not only will Mr Rimmer find it of interest, but I myself require a second hearing if only to discover precisely on how many charges we may effectively prosecute you.'

Maginn scowled like a scolded schoolboy. 'Sir, I don't aim to be in this derned country long enough fer your confounded attorneys to read me my rights. I've a passage booked on the next dern steamer outa Liverpool and if I'm not on it with my pardner's body, my paper will wanna know why.'

'What has happened to Saintly?' Rimmer asked.

'Mr Hodges is regrettably no more,' replied Durston, without sympathy. 'Mr Maginn will tell you why.'

Maginn poured himself more whisky, lit a cigar, and began his tale.

'Hodges and me, we knoo there was some kinda trouble here, on account of we've rummaged considerable in our own city closets and we know all the signs of shamming. Soon as we started in to ask around, folks like Mr Durston here clammed up on us, so we had to go elsewhere for our information. 'Tain't hard to find things out in a city when you kin spend freely. Guess we'd figgered out 'most everything that was happening by the time your notices appeared; they jest signified how big the trouble was. Now, soon as a fellow tells me to keep outa the sewers, why, sir, guess that's the place I aim to be. It was jest a matter of finding a way in.'

'Don't you admire that forthright American approach, Durston?' Rimmer asked.

Durston's expression made needless a reply.

'Now ol' Saintly there, he was a tol'able good actor. He puts on a Limey accent and lays hold of a coupla police uniforms—and fer all your police force is incorruptible, that ain't so hard to do. We dress up and go to a subway in Finsbury that looks kinda quiet. Saintly, he shows some piece of paper to the guard on the entrance, tells him we're a coupla constables sent to make some kinda inspection. That fellow was sure fooled good. Poor ol' Saintly . . .'

Maginn broke off, sniffed dolefully, poured more whisky into his glass and downed it.

'So we went into the sewer. Shucks, we bin in worse places. Ain't nowhere stinks more than the brig of a clipper and we both bin in there a coupla times. So we weren't too dainty-minded. Waal, I reckon we musta walked nigh on two mile. Didn't see nothin' of the rats, though we sure could hear them around us. Then derned if ol' Saintly didn't go skitterin' up some branch sewer on his hands and knees. I was 'bout twenny yards behind him when there was one helluva crack and some kinda girder collapses across the branch. Piece of it comes plump down on Saintly's leg; another bit was left hanging above him. Waal, I gave a mighty heave on the bit that had trapped Saintly and he got his leg out, but fainted clean away with the pain. I let the girder roll back between us and figgered best thing I could do was bring help, so I set off back towards Finsbury. Derned if I didn't git but twenny yards before something made me look back. There, standing over Saintly, are three of the biggest dern rats I ever did see. Nivver heard 'em, yet they were bigger than any 'coon or 'possum and I've hunted both.'

Rimmer, Durston, and I exchanged glances. War-lords. In a group and at close quarters for the first time.

'Now I 'lowed there wasn't no way I could help my pardner right then and there, on account of we weren't carrying any shootin' irons, so I kept watch. Pretty soon ol' Saintly came to, and when he saw those monsters, why, he looked pretty dern sick. The rats jest sat and watched him. I figgered they knoo I was there, but they were having their fun with him and weren't 'bout to bother with me.'

Maginn must have seen the question in our eyes, for he stopped and pulled at his whisky.

'Yes, gennlemen, I mean fun. Them critturs was jest amusing themselves with ol' Saintly, saw it in their eyes. Yessir.'

My mind returned to my first encounter with a war-lord, to the look of almost human hatred that it had flung at me, and to McWhirrie's words, 'intelligence as cruel an' calculatin' as oor ain.'

'Waal,' Maginn continued, 'Saintly couldn't abear it and made a move. First time, he tried to pull himself over to the wall; but they were ready fer him. Jest kinda eased themselves into position so's he was forced to stop. Then he made for the other wall, but they blocked him off agin. Saintly began to lose control of himself; I heard him mumbling all manner of things to himself. He made another go fer the wall but straightways they headed him off; and this time, they went on moving towards him, closing in. One of them dropped out and went to the side of the sewer where the remains of the girder hung. I didn't spot his game at first, until he began scrabbling at the brickwork. Saintly started to

93

blubber then, yelling, 'Leave me be, kin't you?' But they came on at him, muzzles forward, teeth showing. Then I noticed that the girder was coming loose where the third of the critturs was clawing at it, and it dawned on me what they were 'bout. I figgered I was gonna see an execution. The two that were manoeuvring around Saintly stopped when they had forced him back under the girder; then the third reached for it, and, gennlemen, that reach was like a young mountain lion's. The girder collapsed upon Saintly and smashed his head to pulp. I didn't wait to see no more, nossir. I jest went on back till I got to the Finsbury subway and took my story to the police.'

Maginn finished the whisky and eyed us with belligerence.

'Don't try to tell me what we shoulda done, me and Saintly. We knoo there was a risk when we went into the sewer. Why, we bin taking risks 'most all our lives. I couldn't do much to help my pardner at the end, but at least I kin get his body, what's left of it, up outa that hole and bury it somewhere decently. Then I'm gonna take the story that he gave his life fer, and I'm gonna sell it fer the highest price I kin squeeze. Ain't no one gonna stop me.'

'Now, there, Mr Maginn,' Durston murmured, 'you are wrong. You have no story to sell.'

'The hell I ain't,' shouted Maginn, but Rimmer waved him silent.

'You see, Mr Maginn,' Durston continued, 'if you persist in attempting to divulge your experiences publicly, we shall be forced to consider with severity your several contraventions of our regulations. Your impersonation of a police officer, for example, will earn you a sentence sufficient to deprive you of many Thanksgiving dinners. Estimable though your newspaper doubtless is, it can guarantee you no immunity. I do beg you to reconsider your position.' Durston's tone expressed the kindliest concern, but his eyes were devoid of sympathy. 'In the meantime, I shall take steps to recover Mr Hodges' body.'

He left the office and Maginn scowled after him. 'Dern it, no wonder you lost America. I figger he's jest the kinda fellow that thought up the Stamp Act and tried to ram it down our gullets. Well, he ain't ramming nothin' down mine. I mean to publish.'

'Let's talk about it, Maginn,' said Rimmer, 'but not here. There's an excellent hostelry around the corner, we'll go there. Er, Matt,' and as he addressed me, his eyelid flickered, 'there's no need for you to come along. Meet us back here in a couple of hours.'

Five hours passed, however, before I saw Rimmer and Maginn again. They entered Durston's office with excessive deliberation and, more by good fortune than design, found two chairs. At the reek of their breath, Durston flung open his window to the nor'easter outside.

'We shest had an amic—amuc—mucam . . . friendly discushon o' mattersh o' mushool interesht,' explained Maginn, placing one foot after another upon Durston's gleaming mahogany desk and almost falling from his chair in the process. 'I'm grafit—grfti . . . glad to shay that we have reashed a shatshfactory sholushon. Ain't that sho, ol' pardner?' Rimmer gave a confirmatory hiccup. 'An I've resholved not to shay a word, norrerwordmin', 'bout the whole dern bushness,' Maginn continued, 'until I am given permishun from the appr—apper—apeprop . . . from shomeone. Ain't that right, ol' fellow?' He appealed to Rimmer once more, who nodded his head, then groaned. 'In the meantime, you're gonna get ol' Shaintly's body outa the shewer. Poor ol' Shaintly, besht frien' a fellow ever had.' And Maginn reached unsteadily from his chair to extract a handkerchief from Durston's pocket, on which to blow his nose.

Rimmer rose and drew Durston aside. 'One part brandy, one part champagne, two parts port and two madeira, topped off with lemon and cinnamon. Repeat for as long as the victim can take it, but steer clear of it yourself. Best cure for intransigence that I know. You owe me three pounds. Now, for goodness sake, find that body. Matt, you go with him. I'm going to bed.'

We left Maginn snoring under the surveillance of Durston's clerks and sent Rimmer home in a cab. Then Durston took me to the river beside Blackfriars Bridge. He

95

explained that from Maginn's description of his sewer and the journey along it, Bazalgette's engineers had identified the place where Hodges' body had been left; but on entering that part of the sewer, they had found a chasm where the body should have been and had guessed that the fall of the girder had led to the collapse of the sewer. They had calculated that Hodges' body would have fallen into a system of low level sewers and hence to one of the river outlets, and had searched there also. When the corpse had still not been found, watermen had suggested that the tide had washed it out and that it might have caught upon the staunchions of old Blackfriars Bridge, then in the process of being demolished, or on those of the temporary bridge that had been erected alongside. To find out, Durston had ordered a diver to explore the piles of the bridges and, if the body were there, to free it and bring it to the surface.

Christmas Night had fallen; but over the bridges the sky was yellowed by the glow of a thousand naptha-lamps, as the demolition continued around the clock. Silhouetted against the glare was a row of skeletal machines, each powered from a squat boiler.

'Steam-cranes,' said Durston. 'They run upon rails along the top of the scaffolding around the bridges and carry blocks of masonry wherever they are needed. They lack elegance, but save time and labour, and are therefore, in an age where economy comes before art, much admired.'

The diver and his crew stood in a knot at the edge of an outcrop of scaffolding. I never discovered the diver's name, since he was constantly referred to as the Manxman. He was a small man, dark and sombre, who returned curt answers to Durston's questions. Over a vest and drawers of flannel, he wore a waterproof costume, something like a jacket and trousers made in one; on top of this lay his breastplate, with an india-rubber binding, and there were india-rubber bands tight upon his wrists; on his head he wore a woollen nightcap. Having tightened the butterfly-headed nuts upon his breastplate, he snapped an order to the crew, who eased his feet into boots, soled, said Durston, with an inch of lead; next, they hung two 50 lb weights before and behind; and, finally, they settled a spherical helmet over his head, fastened it to the breastplate and proceeded to tighten every nut. On a last command, the mouthpiece was closed, and the diver prepared to descend, clambering over the edge of the scaffolding, lifeline carefully payed out behind him.

'He can stay down for an hour,' said Durston. 'He'll need every minute if the body cannot readily be freed.'

'But it's so cold,' I expostulated.

Durston shook his head. 'It makes little difference to a diver whether it's hot or cold; his hands will be numbed by the rubber wristbands. He is accustomed to working without a proper sense of touch.'

We stood looking down into the oily pool, watching the lifeline move back and forth for half an hour; then we heard one of the crew shout, 'There! That's the signal. 'Ee's fahnd the corpus.'

A set of weighted cables was lowered and within twenty minutes a dripping bundle was hauled up on to the scaffolding. While we were arranging for the dispatch of Hodges' remains to a mortuary, however, there was a buzz of concern amongst the crew. Durston joined them and asked the reason. The Manxman had signalled distress, he was told. A standby diver stripped off his guernsey, gulped in air, and plunged into the river. He surfaced eventually to call to us that in freeing Hodges, the Manxman had dislodged a beam, which had fallen on his foot and trapped it. He was still breathing, said the standby, but had less than ten minutes to go. The beam, he added, was too heavy to shift manually; some other means must be found. The crew argued among themselves and Durston watched impatiently as seconds were wasted. At last, he rejoined the men and urged some scheme upon them—I could not hear his voice above the clatter from the demolition squads—causing them to shake their heads, then ultimately to concur. He returned to my side.

'A possibility, no more,' he said. 'I've suggested that they use one of the steam-cranes to haul the timber away.'

Moments later, there came a whistle and one of the machines edged along its track until its head hovered directly over the point where the diver was trapped. There were earnest conferences between the crew and the engineer; then, with a rattle, the crane's cables snaked down into the water. The standby plunged again and attached the claw-grip to the fallen timber. A signal was passed to the engineer, the whistle shrilled once more, and the cables were withdrawn with a chilling shriek. The water boiled suddenly and from it came the beam, to be swung up and over our heads on to the scaffolding above. Soon afterwards the Manxman surfaced. He had escaped one minute before his time expired. As the crew removed his suit, they spoke to him and pointed to Durston. The Manxman made no reply, but sat chafing the blue flesh where the rubber had compressed his wrists; then he dressed and made to leave, as uncommunicative after his escape from death as he had been before his dive. Only as he departed, did he turn in our direction and give a brusque nod of acknowledgement.

'Rum fellow,' I remarked in my most Rimmer-like tones. 'Had a lot to say for himself, didn't he?'

'I should have thought,' murmured my companion, 'that he considers the strain of his occupation sufficient, without adding to it the ponderous weight of your raillery.' He paused and the acidity left his voice. 'To awake each morning, wondering if that day's descent will bring death . . .' (Durston was talking to himself now, oppressed by some private concern) 'to awake each morning and take up the same heavy burden . . .' He caught my eye upon him and regained his habitual arrogant languor. 'We must return to the redoubtable Maginn, who will, I trust, be suitably chastened by the after-effects of his libations.' He hailed a hansom, composed once more. But for a moment I had glimpsed another Durston, a man whose mind was racked by anxiety. By fear. Or was it by guilt?

Durston put me down from his cab at Little Newport Street and I entered our rooms to find Pride and Passion serving weak tea to Rimmer, who looked much the worse for his conference with Maginn, and eyed the anaemic brew with distaste.

'There's nothing wrong with me that a glass of port won't

cure,' I heard him protest.

'Nonsense!' said his servitor. 'You are intemperate to a degree that ill becomes an older man.'

A blasphemous retort to this reference to Rimmer's age was only averted by my arrival. Rimmer made it the excuse to slide his cup away; he later surreptitiously emptied its contents into a bucket.

'Miss Tiptree brings us news of a fresh sign of popular hysteria,' he explained. 'A wave of evangelism is sweeping through the rookeries and she fears that it may have deadly repercussions upon our plans.'

'Come and see for yourselves,' Pride and Passion invited; and Rimmer, anxious to avoid a further brew of tea, readily obeyed.

We returned to St Giles, and Pride and Passion led us through a maze of streets near her mission to a stretch of open ground, where there stood a tent around which a crowd was milling. Its weather-stained exterior was hung with texts painted in red upon yellow sheets of pasteboard.

'Blessed is he that readeth, and they that hear, the words of this prophecy, for the time is at hand,' asserted one.
'Repent or else I will come to thee quickly and will fight,' warned a second.
'Woe to the inhabiters of the earth,' menaced a fourth; adding in explanation, 'for the devil is come down to you having great wrath.'

We joined the queueing congregation and shuffled with it into the steamy interior. Ramshackle benches were set out in rows and four deacons, greeting each arrival with unctuous good-fellowship as 'brother' or 'sister', methodically filled every space upon them.

'To which denomination do we owe this evening's entertainment?' Rimmer asked.

'The New, Reformed and United Calvinist Congregation of the Gospel, brother,' replied a deacon and handed Rimmer a leaflet which announced that the Reverend Zephaniah Eden would that night bring balm unto bruised breasts and sweet succour to suffering souls.

'More damned alliteration,' complained Rimmer when he had read it. 'Evangelistic preachers are no less susceptible to it than radical politicians.'

A bell clanged to announce the start of the service and the house-lights, two rows of smokey candles, were extinguished, leaving an illuminated circle at one end of the tent. Into it stepped a minor prophet. Not, admittedly, in sackcloth and ashes, or raiment rent in despair; in fact, he was clad in a greasy coat, with soiled cuffs and oily collar. But the sunken face and emaciated limbs were those of one who had not seen manna for a week and had passed a good deal of time under withered fig-trees; the eyes glowed with revelation and the Mancunian voice was hoarse with prophecy.

'Brothers, brothers and sisters, brothers and sisters, great and small, all God's children, children all, I bring tidings to you; tidings of great joy to those amongst you that are cleansed in the blood of the Lamb, born this day to bring redemption; tidings of woe to you sinners that quake beneath His footstool. For I have seen, yea, I have seen such things as only the elect may see; and I have been called to bear witness to you all, that the Lord is merciful to them that beg His forgiveness, but mighty in His wrath to them that skulk in the night and turn their faces from Him. For lo! a time is at hand when He shall pass among His flock and carry His lambs to a sweeter pasture; but the sinners shall be cast into the forest and shall become the prey of the Beast. Hallelujah!'

A number of crones in the front stalls echoed his cry with such vehemence that their bonnets slipped askew and their prayer books clattered to the ground. While they retrieved them, the Reverend Zephaniah called for a carol and one of the deacons struck up a tune upon a portable harmonium propped against one of the tent-poles. I did not recognize the refrain, but it appeared to be a favourite with the front row, which sang with vigour and lingered regretfully over the final note. Prayers followed, making up in fervour what they lacked in grammar, and more carols. I could see nothing alarming in the demeanour of preacher or preached-at, and Rimmer was sufficiently unconcerned to have fallen into a doze. But as a fourth carol ended and the deacons escorted their pastor to a railed dais that served as a pulpit, I became aware of a stirring in the congregation. I nudged Rimmer, who awoke in time to catch a meaning glance from Pride and Passion.

'My text,' began the Reverend Zephaniah, 'I take not from the Gospels, which tell of the first coming of Our Lord, but from the Book of Revelations, wherein we learn of His second coming. "There came out of the smoke, locusts upon the earth; and unto them was given power." ' He drew breath and launched himself into a farrago of nonsense that anywhere else would have reduced an audience to mirth, but which, in that dark, stifling tent, amid the drumming of hail and sleet upon the canvas and the moaning of the wind in the roof, became only too believable. The second coming, he asserted, was at hand. The signs were about us: the multitudes that lived in want; the spread of sickness and desolation; the rivalry of nation with nation that could end only in Armageddon; and—here he leant out over his congregation so that it shrank back under his vehemence— the coming among us of beasts. For had not the prophet foretold that at the end of the world would come locusts that would stalk the earth and have dominion over all, so that in those days men should seek death, so great would be their torment? Yea, thus had he spoken. But he was a prophet of the East, where the locust was the common harrier of the tribes of Asia and Asia Minor. So what of the western world, where the locust was no hazard? Would it, then, escape damnation? Assuredly not; for thither would the Lord send the counterpart of the locust: a beast that consumed the food of men, lived off their plenty, lurked in their houses and prayed betimes upon their bodies. What was this beast? The Reverend Zephaniah reached from his dais into a darkened recess and held over the heads of a shrieking front row a wicker cage of rats.

'These, brothers; these, sisters; these are the beasts that have been sent to torment us; this is the plague with which we have been visited at our end; these are the brutes that shall hold such sway over us that we shall crave death in order to

101

escape their domination. Yea, truly they are among us now, though government and vestryman dare not say so. The day of Apollyon is at hand and these are his harbingers, creeping from the sewers to tear the flesh from our bones.'

The cage swung hypnotically from his hand. He dropped his voice and crooned to his congregation. All, he told us, was not lost. The Lord had given to him, and to others of the elect, the power to go down into the bottomless, smoking pit, whence came the beasts upon us, there to wrestle with them, and with God's grace, to overcome. Behold! His voice rising to a shriek, the preacher tore open the cage and, seizing one of the rats, brandished it high above his head and broke its spine on the rails of his dais. Then another. And another. His deacons imitated him, grabbing at the rats and snapping their necks. The crones of the front row, screaming incoherently, joined them. Soon the entire congregation was milling around the dais, snatching the rats' bodies and ripping them apart.

Pride and Passion turned to us. 'It won't be long before he leads them underground,' she said. 'He believes he has the power to do it; and he will take his converts with him. You remember what happened the last time a mob went down?'

An image of columns of fire from a blazing gas main caused me to shudder. 'He must be stopped,' I cried.

'He will be,' said Rimmer grimly. 'I'll get Durston to confine him under some by-law.'

'But what about the others?' asked Pride and Passion. 'There are at least six branches of this sect in central London alone, all preaching the same message.'

'We'll close them down, too,' vowed Rimmer.

We left the tent and returned to the mission hall.

'No matter what you do to the preachers,' said Pride and Passion, 'the poor will still be frightened. Did you know that many of them are selling their houses and rooms and leaving St Giles? I've heard the same from other slums.'

This was news to us, disquieting news at that. Twenty families had left houses near the mission, she told us, in the last six days; and more were intending to leave the following week. They were selling for whatever they could get; the prices were usually pitifully low.

'Someone,' asserted Pride and Passion, 'is preying on the fear and ignorance of the poor to make a fortune from the menace of the rats.'

VII
Behind the lines

It was nine o'clock on Christmas Night when we returned to Little Newport Street. McWhirrie and Gunn had let themselves in and had spread a noble supper of goose, plum pudding, and mince pies upon the table. Eyeing it, Rimmer remarked coldly that Gunn's aunt, our proveditor, was evidently a staunch adherent of Mr Dickens' belief that the season should not pass unmarked by sentimentality and indigestion; nevertheless, he ate his share and more of the fowl and beat McWhirrie to the last mince pie. After which, we roasted chestnuts and planned our route into the sewers of Hungerford Market, where, declared Rimmer, as prone to the novelletish cliché as I, the truth lay hidden.

Gunn had brought with him several portfolios of plans, which he had borrowed from the offices of the Board of Works, and we studied those that covered the market site. The building of Charing Cross railway station and hotel there, had been preceded by a detailed subterranean survey; but to our astonishment, it showed no drains constructed earlier than the thirties of this century and was of no use to us. Scud arrived, bringing with him Mrs Scud's festive greetings and a brew of the most potent negus that ever scalded gullet. He knelt over the plans with us, saying that he had asked among his tosher friends but had found none that knew of old sewers in the vicinity of Hungerford. Discouraged, we turned to a sheaf of older plans, several of them from the early eighteenth century, and strove to decipher the florid script in their rococo cartouches.

'Fit's 'at?' asked McWhirrie, retrieving a faded sheet that Gunn had dismissed as uninformative, and pointing to a wavering line that emerged from a patch of mould at the bottom of the plan. The line skirted Hungerford and ran to an outlet on the shore of the Thames at Westminster.

'It could be the line of an early sewer,' Gunn admitted, and began a search in plans of a later date to identify it. Although we scanned every plan that Gunn had brought, however, we could find no trace of it; only in the recent survey did we discover a sewer that followed its course, running from the river outlet for about half a mile before veering off in a totally different direction.

'We'll investigate it, nevertheless,' Rimmer declared.

'Ai know the outlet to the river,' said Scud. 'Ai saw it whin we were draivin' pailes for the embankment. Theer will be caissons sunk in front of it now. 'Twon't be aisy tew enter.'

'We'll take that chance.' Rimmer hesitated. 'Should we inform Durston, d'ye think?'

'Nae fear,' McWhirrie was adamant.

Gunn supported him. 'Officially, the Army is in control. Durston would have to report our intentions to that egregious ass Crashaw, who would be bound to interfere.'

Scud added his plea. 'Yon sojer brings nothin' but disaster, sor. Hivven knows what plan he's concocted these past tew days. Let's jist keep clear av him, whaile we may.'

'Motion carried, *nem. con.*,' ruled Rimmer, and packed McWhirrie and Gunn off to Hammersmith, their protests notwithstanding. Scud, he invited to stay the night; our comrade, anticipating the invitation, had brought his nightshirt and a bolster.

'Get a good night's rest,' Rimmer advised, distributing the last of the negus. He fished out another one from the novelette: 'We start at dawn.'

A red dawn smeared with cirrus it was, and the waters of the Thames were stained with blood. The tide was out and we descended greasy steps at Horseferry to splash in our long boots across the mud below the Houses of Parliament and into the embankment workings. They were deserted: the labourers were sleeping off their Christmas potations in the camp hovels and no work was being done that morning. Scud now conducted us, by way of scaffolding, duckboards, plank bridges, perilous timber rafts, and the rims of sunken caissons, to the point where he had seen the outlet which he believed to correspond with that marked on our plan. We were fortunate: it had not been blocked, although a caisson stood near, ready to be anchored in front of it. There was just enough room for Scud and me to squeeze past the iron frame and through the grill that hung askew at the mouth of the outlet, but we had to manoeuvre Rimmer into place like two tugs with a schooner. We shone our bull's-eyes on the brickwork of the interior. Beneath their dense coating of filth and slime, the bricks were small and brown; eighteenth-century, speculated Rimmer, possibly earlier. This was undoubtedly the sewer on our early plan, but did it run to Hungerford?

'There's but one way to find out,' Rimmer announced and, lapsing into French to suit his heroic mood, exclaimed with a gesture, '*En avant, mes braves!*' and hit his head on the roof.

We made slow work of it. The sewer ran on an incline, with a deep channel and many twists and turns. Sewage gushed up to our calves, sometimes to our thighs, and we were grateful to Scud for providing us with steel-pointed staves such as the toshers used; these alone saved us from losing our precarious balance. Rimmer had brought with him Gunn's two plans and wrestled with their flapping sections in growing exasperation. Suddenly he halted us. It was here, according to the plans, he explained, that the lines of the early and recent sewer diverged. He set us to find corroborating evidence in the structure of the tunnel, and we found it. Ten yards or so ahead, the bricks became large and yellow, the crust of dirt upon them thinner. There, declared Rimmer, ran the modern sewer, its builders evidently having economized by utilizing the lowest section of its predecessor. Was this, then, the end of the early one? A single, disagreeable, course of action presented itself; and he led us in an onslaught upon the matted filth that festooned the walls, tearing down swathes of the stuff to leave the early brickwork clear.

It was Scud who found the answer. He and I had just wrenched off a strip of rotting vegetation to lay bare a patch

106

of brick, when his darting eyes caught something that mine had missed, and he called for all three lanterns to bear upon it. Faintly incised across a stone set among the bricks was the legend

WEST^r COMM^{rs} OF SEWERS, BY ORDER, 1723

Rimmer scraped at the moss still adhering to the wall and traced the pattern of the mortar. Then I saw what he was searching for: the regular, alternating array of lines was broken by a transverse arc, which, as Rimmer clawed away further wedges of moss, assumed the outline of an upper invert. The old sewer had been blocked. Behind this barrier, we surmised, it followed its original course to Hungerford.

'Gunn should be able to discover the reason for the barrier,' commented Rimmer. 'He knows his way about the records of the Westminster Commissioners and, with a date to help him, it should be simple. As for us, gentlemen, do we ignore the commissioners' order and go on?'

In reply, Scud inserted the tip of his stave between two bricks and bore down upon it. Mortar fell to the ground. Without further speech we joined him and demolished the barrier. When the sound of rending brickwork had ceased and the dust and dirt had settled, we stepped over the rubble into a tunnel undisturbed by man for a century and more.

The dryness was what we noticed first. The stream of sewage that had once coursed along the sewer had long since been extinguished. There was no incessant gurgle, no rhythmic dripping of water, no humid growth upon the walls. But there was still a stench, not of sewage now, but an animal odour, the smell of a shambles in a market, of blood, entrails, and ordure; and there was a noise, high-pitched, incessant, but too faint to recognize. As we stumbled forwards, my boot struck something that chinked. I picked up a coin, and Rimmer, bending his single eye upon it, whistled, 'A shilling-piece. Two heads. William and Mary. Well, well, what other treasures will we find?'

The question may have been rhetorical, but it was answered in actuality. The further we explored the old sewer, the greater the number, and the stranger the nature, of the objects that lay scattered under our feet; objects which, as Scud explained, must once have been carried in the sewage, but which had been left stranded when the stream had dried up. Coins there were by the purseful: silver groats of the Restoration, a Protectorate penny, a Jacobean crown and a Tudor noble; scrutinizing the last, Rimmer reminded us that the site of Hungerford Market had formerly been occupied by the town house of the Hungerford family. No further explanation was necessary, for a variety of domestic articles—crested spoons, a sword-hilt, gilded tongs curiously wrought, and a silver salt that Cellini might have fashioned—revealed that the sewer in which we stood was of older origin than the eighteenth century and, as an open ditch, had probably drained the Hungerfords' mansion in the days of Elizabeth. We were more puzzled by the number of French *écus* and *louis d'or* which we discovered, until Rimmer recalled that Huguenots, seeking shelter in England from the persecution of the French king, had worshipped together in a building on the Hungerford property.

We had forgotten the purpose of our visit and our guard had dropped. When we raised our heads from the articles strewn about us and saw a war-lord mere feet from us, we thought neither of defence nor flight but looked dumbly upon him as he bared his teeth, hunched, and sprang. Rimmer, preceding us, took the weight of the charge upon his leather jerkin and gauntleted hands, and was felled by the shock; but the beast found no tooth-hold in the greasy leather and retreated, to turn, check, and charge again. Rimmer struggled to his knees.

'Remember Crécy!' he shouted, an injunction totally lost on Scud and myself.

But we saw that, still kneeling, he had regained his stave and had wedged it, point outwards, against his foot. We imitated him in time to present to our assailant a row of points, uneven, but sufficient to skewer the rat in the breast as he sprang again. We dragged our weapons from the carcass and arose; at which stage, I recalled my engravings for a series of *Noble Victories of English Arms* and informed Rimmer that the hedge of stakes had been at Agincourt, not

108

Crécy. The point was not well taken and I did not pursue it.

Why, we wondered, had the war-lòrd challenged us so impetuously? What was he guarding? And where were the packs that usually did the war-lords' fighting for them? We took the next turning of the sewer and found the explanation.

Before us there were branch-sewers; none had been indicated on Gunn's plans, but from right and left ran a score of branches, few of them wider than large water-pipes. From them was emitted the stench that we had noticed on entering the sewer, but doubled in strength, so that, though we clapped hands to our noses and mouths, we choked and retched repeatedly. The noise, too, was magnified; a ceaseless squealing, squeaking, mewling, and puling, so distorted by the acoustics of the pipes that our heads throbbed with it and our minds swam. Scud stretched out at the entrance to one of the branches, peered into it, then wriggled to another, and so for twenty or thirty yards along the tunnel. He returned and motioned to us to do as he had done. I saw nothing in the first two branches—indeed, so noisome were they, in both senses, that I could barely press my face to them. But in the third I saw what Scud had seen and shared his incredulity. For I was looking into a nursery.

The branch had been widened at its farther end and opened into a broad chamber, of which I could see but a small segment. Its floor was layered with rags—tatters of brocaded coats, strands of sprigged muslin, shreds of broadcloth, with, here and there, a froth of lace. I had engraved enough 'period pieces' to discern in the frayed and rotting finery fragments of fashions that had bedecked the inhabitants of Hungerford House and had been draped upon the stalls of Hungerford Market—slashed doublets, quilted breeches, farthingales, and saques. The occupants of the chamber wriggled, rolled, fought or lay at ease upon its lining: pink, naked ratlings, babies and infants, beyond all doubt the most obscene sight I have ever beheld. The soft, wrinkled flesh, the pale redness around the eyes, the pliant limbs, and quivering snouts, in tiny creatures might have implied vulnerability and have evoked pity or affection in

109

response. But these were not tiny creatures, they were the size of small pigs, bloated, and full gorged; and there was a cruelty, a spite, in their play, which made me think of pampered bullies at a public school. The noise and smell overcame me and I retreated to the middle of the sewer where Rimmer and Scud were awaiting me.

'It's the quantity of them that frightens me,' Rimmer was saying. 'I had imagined that the war-lords were few in number, a highly exclusive strain. But this is obviously their breeding-ground and I counted a good fifty ratlings—lordlings, I suppose we should call them—within my own limited field of vision. Multiply that many times and you have a generation numerous enough to dominate every sewer in London.'

'Did they construct the nursery themselves?' I asked, for I now believed the war-lords capable of anything.

Rimmer shook his head. 'The Hungerford site has been built upon since the Middle Ages,' he explained. 'I suspect that the chamber was once the cellar of a medieval hall.'

'An' wheer would all the ornery rats be, thin?' asked Scud.

'Strictly confined to their own nests and warrens, I should think,' Rimmer replied. 'The war-lords' domain seems to be patrolled by their own kind. They probably believe in caste and the purity of their race, and intend to preserve their strain intact, like certain backward tribes—the English aristocracy for one.'

A scuffling in the tunnel, sensed rather than heard over the din from the nursery, drew me back to investigate. Two more war-lords, or rather, their ladies, had appeared. They were dismembering the corpse that we had left behind us. Each had her brood beside her and was encouraging it to try its teeth upon the severed limbs. The war-lords, I had discovered, carried the concept of racial purity to a drastic, if logical, conclusion. I returned to warn Rimmer that once the ladies had finished their butchery, they would come after us, or dispatch further sentinels in our pursuit. He led us forward, past the remaining nursery branches, and into a section of the old sewer, so narrow that we were forced to worm our way along it; how much further we could have

110

travelled in this manner I do not know, but the increasing volume of Rimmer's imprecations suggested that one worm, at least, was about to turn. Our journey ended abruptly, however, when the floor collapsed beneath us, and we somersaulted and spiralled many feet downwards, to arrive in a blasphemous pile at the bottom of a pit; lumps of masonry followed us, and only that special deity, responsible for the welfare of one-eyed men with a taste for port, preserved Rimmer's skull (which surmounted our scrimmage) from fragmentation. We were familiar by now with the tendency of the rotten brickwork of London sewers to disintegrate at inappropriate moments; it was in consequence of one such fall that I had had my first encounter with a rat-pack, and following another that the sanctified Hodges had met his end. But it was this third collapse that was to have the most unusual outcome.

We picked ourselves up and investigated the various pains that we had begun to register, distinguishing where we could between lacerations, bruises, and breaks. I felt as if I had gone twelve rounds with Tom Cribb, bare knuckles, kicking and gouging not disbarred; and Rimmer and Scud, when I shone my bull's-eye upon them, also looked as if they had suffered at the fists of a couple of Regency prize-fighters.

'Well,' said Scud—I think he had been dipping into our novellette—'no bones broken.'

'Not ours, at least,' replied Rimmer and the tone of his voice distracted my attention from my aching ribs.

We had fallen beyond man-made workings into a natural fissure, and Rimmer was scrutizing its gently tapering walls. Apart from the fact that they were unscaleable save by an Alpine guide or his goat, I could see nothing remarkable about them, and Rimmer's mutterings in no way enlightened me.

'Sandy clay, about three to four feet—clay and pebbles, a foot—greyish sand, I suppose about nine inches—yellow clayish sand, nearly a foot—clay with flints, a good two feet—gravel and flints, three feet at least—and then clay, sand and ironstone, nine to ten feet.'

111

His light eventually returned to, and rested upon, a particular section of the far wall, and I saw at last what it was that preoccupied him. Embedded in the earth was a bone. Scud saw it too.

'In Heaven's name, sor, what would that be, now?'

'Difficult to be certain,' answered Rimmer, 'but my guess is that it's a metacarpal.' My gaping jaw prompted a further explanation. 'A bone between the forearm and the hand.'

'A man's?'

'Good lord, no! An elephant's.'

'An elephant's!' breathed Scud.

'*Elephas antiquus*, to be precise,' asserted Rimmer, being precise. 'Owen has two at the British Museum, both from Essex, if I'm not mistaken.' He roared at our bewilderment and, with a happy disregard for our predicament—trapped in a pit in hostile territory—lit his pipe and proceeded to explain himself and to introduce us at the same time to the subject of paleontology.

It had been in India, during the Mutiny, that Rimmer had first been introduced to the study of extinct animals. He had saved a young official of the East India Company from a particularly unpleasant death at the hands of some renegade sepoys and, while he was trying to plug some of the superfluous holes that they had made in their victim, he had discovered in the man's pocket a fragment of bone in an envelope addressed to a Dr Hugh Falconer in England. The official had not regained consciousness and Rimmer had assumed the responsibility of delivering the bone on the dead man's behalf. It was thus that he had met Falconer, the renowned expert upon mastodons, mammoths, and elephants. The paleontologist had thanked him warmly for his trouble, had explained that the official had been a pupil who had accompanied him upon many digs in India, and had shown Rimmer a study filled with bones and casts of bones from which he was reconstructing the history of the elephant and its ancestors. Within two hours he had made a convert and Rimmer had returned to London to buy all the books he could find on the subject—I recalled the geological quarterlies on which I had propped my feet during my first

112

night at Little Newport Street—and had become sufficiently expert to have identified a third left upper true molar of an *Elephas meridionalis* in a handful of fragments for sale in a New York market. Now he was sure that he had found a metacarpal and did not dare guess at what might lie beside it. He was so overwhelmed by excitement that, to my astonishment and Scud's exasperation, he borrowed my sketch-book and began a set of careful drawings of the wretched bit of antiquated jumbo.

'Tell yew what, sor,' said Scud, anxious to speed his labour, 'Ai'll get it out av theer for ye in a jiffy.'

He inserted his stave under the tip of the bone, but Rimmer hauled him away, horrified, and dared him to go near it again. It was essential, he explained, that we should leave the bone exactly as we had found it; then, when we had done for the rats, we could return with McWhirrie—'He's a fossil fish man when he has time'—and Gunn—'He once set Huxley right about a skull'—and, of course, Owen—'Best comparative anatomist alive'—to make a detailed survey of the site and begin an excavation.

'That's all very well, sor,' interrupted Scud, 'but jist how dew we take the good news back tew them. Ai've bin lewking at this pit an' Ai can't for the laife av me see a way of escape. Ai've a bit av rope around me waist, but 'tis no use tew us unless one av us is aloft to make it safe.'

My spirits, which had risen as Rimmer had spoken with such confidence of a ratless future, sank once more; I was about to cry hysterically, with my habitual novelettish response, that all was lost, when Rimmer scraped out his pipe and remarked nonchalantly that it was clear that Scud had never escaped from a Chinese dungeon. No, said Scud, he hadn't had that experience, him never having fancied the Orient, though he was partial to its tea. Rimmer, becoming the inscrutable Sinologist and muttering to himself in Mandarin, borrowed Scud's knife and sharpened the unshod ends of our staves. At length, he deigned to enlighten us between strokes:

'China—during the war—some damned princeling put six of us—war correspondents, d'ye see—into the deepest dungeon—in his palace—beastly great pit—twice as deep as this—well, one of our fellows borrowed three canes—tiny chap, he was, French, but one of the decent ones—and simply chaired himself to the top. I will now,' he continued, brandishing the staves with the air of a Maskelyne, 'demonstrate the technique with the assistance of any young gentleman from the audience.' And he drew me forward by the ear.

The discerning reader may not have formed too high an estimate of my talents in the course of this narrative. My role had, until this point, been largely confined to looking on, asking inane questions, entangling myself in situations from which others had to come to my rescue, and fainting when things became too much for me. Now, it seemed, Rimmer had perceived in me some innate heroic quality, and I was determined to prove worthy of his trust. I was mortified, therefore, to discover subsequently that he had chosen me for my size.

Following Rimmer's instructions, I stood upon a large piece of masonry and scraped grooves in the earthen sides of the pit, which were, near its base, almost cylindrical; into them I set two of the staves, like horizontal bars, forming a chord across a shallow arc; balancing on these, I took the third stave and inserted it in the same fashion at eye level; I then hoisted myself into a sitting position upon it and, using my feet as levers and hoist, drew up my first two staves and repeated the procedure. It was only near the top, where the walls began to diverge sharply, that I experienced any difficulty; one of the two staves, by then barely covering the distance, fell from its groove, and I very nearly joined it in its descent. I retained my seat, however, and, on Rimmer's bellowed instructions, shortened the arc and chord; in this way I reached the brim and heaved myself into the tunnel once more. I made fast Scud's rope and tossed the end to its owner, who had piled broken masonry from the pit to form a column; balancing upon its tip, he was just able to seize the rope and pull himself up to join me. When Rimmer's turn came, however, he had but set foot upon the top of the pillar when it gave way beneath his weight; he grabbed the rope in time to save himself from a second descent, but was left swinging helplessly. His pendulating body strained the rope and its anchor, and Scud and I were forced to take it around our waists; in doing so we jolted our burden, widening his swing, so that he touched the side below us and was able to convert his momentum into a run, which carried him to the top and brought us to within three inches of the edge.

'An interlude of unexpected interest,' he declared, when we had recovered breath and strength. 'Now let's find a way out of this warren.'

Our exertions had driven from my mind, again, the plight in which we had originally found ourselves; now, remembering that we were only a little way beyond the nursery, still at the mercy of the war-lords' sentinels, and far from any outlet into the main system of sewers, my courage returned to its customary low level and I resumed my serpentine progress, nose six inches from Rimmer's heels. As we put yards between ourselves and the fissure, however, the tunnel widened until we were able to regain our feet; there were no more branches and sound and smell diminished to tolerable levels. As I marked the configuration of the walls, I noticed that the masonry had changed: brick had been replaced by stone; stone, moreover, that bore traces of rudimentary carving. I was, therefore, not surprised when Rimmer halted to suggest that we now found ourselves in the medieval foundations of the Hungerford mansion, and that what we had originally thought of as an eighteenth-century sewer had as its origin the channel that drained a fourteenth-century cellar.

We did not have long in which to indulge our feudal fancies; no sooner had we perceived that the cellar was, in fact, a series of low-roofed, barrel-vaulted, open-ended rooms, forming a single, extensive concourse, and that at one end the vaulting had collapsed to leave a high mound of rubble, than Scud, whose ear was ever alert for the sound of rats, motioned us to immediate silence, then sent us scurrying to the heap and pulled us into hiding behind a barricade of fractured masonry. We were barely in position before we felt the stone vibrate beneath us, heard the running of rats as we had never heard it before, and saw the flagged floor vanish under a carpet of brown, which heaved and strained as if lifted by a hundred thousand draughts.

It was as I watched the rats assemble below us that I understood for the first time the magnitude of the task we had set ourselves: not simply in terms of their number, though this was daunting enough, but in terms of their organization and discipline. Although they seemed at first a shifting, restless mass, it was not long before I discerned patterns in their arrangement: packs remained distinct from one another, with as little confraternity, Rimmer whispered to me, as a Highland regiment flanking a Lowland; each had its own war-lord and was ranged behind him in order of size; one pack was composed entirely, so it seemed, of runts, and I wondered if these had been the scavengers that Mrs Lynch had seen ten days ago in Perseverance Place. But we had more still to learn of the hierarchy of the warrens. On an instant, the war-lords gave a single cry in unison, the jostling ceased, and the rats squatted silently. Into the cellar came a group of war-lords, but not such as we had seen before. Venerable beasts, these, who dragged their great weight along wearily but with dignity. I had learned from McWhirrie enough to distinguish an old rat from a young, but I had never imagined that the signs of age could be so marked and an animal yet active: some of the newcomers were blind, others moved stiffly, others still showed in their coats the ravages of sickness; yet all were venerated by the packs and their leaders, who parted to make a way for them.

'I suspect that these are the elders of the warrens,' whispered Rimmer, 'the wise men, if you prefer it, or the war council. It is from here that they direct the strategy of the packs, I imagine, leaving the war-lords to decide upon tactics.'

An hour passed and his conclusions were proved correct, as far as we could judge without McWhirrie there to interpret movements, gestures, and sounds for us. The elders debated, the war-lords transmitted their decisions to the packs, and the rank-and-file sat mute. Until, that is, the war-lords cried again, whereupon the entire population of the cellar began

116

the hypnotic writing that I had witnessed in my first encounter with the rats, a motion that transfixed my eyes once more, so that Rimmer had to jerk hard at my arm before I would attend to him.

'They are on the offensive again,' he whispered. 'Heaven knows what has set them off. It can't be our presence because we've left no witnesses to it.'

'Ai reckon someone's gone and disobeyed Mr Durston's orders,' Scud opined.

'Then we'd better get out quickly and give a warning,' I hissed. 'But how?'

'We'll follow the packs when they leave,' said Rimmer. 'At a safe distance.'

They were beginning to leave now. A decision had been reached, it seemed, orders had been issued, the army had been incited, and the packs were departing in a purposeful manner. I prayed that we would reach the surface before they went into action.

The cellar was empty and we descended from our hiding-place, as we thought, in safety. But we were not alone: one of the elders had remained, squatting in a corner, indistinct against the dark stone. He gave a throaty cry of warning and two sentinels came to his aid. They did not attack at once, as their comrade had in our earlier duel, but circled us out of range of the staves with which we lunged at them, detaining us effectively until they should be reinforced. Scud knew that we could not afford the delay. Hefting his stave like a javelin, he launched it at one of the sentinels, who, pre-occupied with Rimmer's lunges, took it full in the throat. Without pause, Scud snatched my stave and took aim once more, catching the second beast a blow on the haunch that knocked him sideways and gave Rimmer the chance to finish him off.

'Not unlike pig-sticking in India,' Rimmer was saying, as we withdrew our staves, when we heard Scud call for help.

The elder, whom we had imagined too frail to participate in the fight, had sprung upon Scud and had borne him down before we could intervene, his teeth deep into Scud's neck, clinging long after we had smashed his spine.

117

Scud lay before us, his jaw set; poison, the distillation of every kind of foulness from the beast's stinking muzzle, spreading through his body. Rimmer pulled off his kerchief, the nearest thing to clean linen that we had, and staunched the wound. Scud lost consciousness under his ministrations and Rimmer took the chance to tell me that the injury was grave and that we must find a way out of the warren as soon as we could. Humping the inert Scud between us, we took the most spacious passage from the hall, striking northwards as far as we could judge. It proved to be a wise choice. When we had covered about half a mile and were almost done for—Scud, though a small man, was heavy—our burden awoke.

'Lay me down,' he commanded, 'and let me listen.' Blood streamed again from his punctured neck as he cocked his head to one side. 'Forther along, jist a wee bit, now, see if there's a gully.'

There was, indeed; and as we drew near to it, my own ears heard what Scud's had caught at a distance—the gurgle of flowing sewage. Rimmer and I took our staves and launched ourselves at the tunnel walls; they were once again of brick and under our frantic efforts flakes fell away, a crevice appeared, and, finally, we were able to prise away a large piece of masonry and entered a sewer of tolerable size. It took me only minutes to recognize some of its features—manhole marked 12, bricks in the shape of a dog, iron girder with an L-shaped crack—features that Scud had taught me to memorize when he had first brought me here. We were in the Covent Garden sewer and it was not long before we were on our way to the King Street subway.

Scud's ears heard more than sewage, however; we were still some distance from the manhole that would lead us to safety, when he bade us stop again. We laid him down, he cocked his head as before, and pointed southwards. We listened with him and at last distinguished a regular, muffled thumping.

Scud's voice was barely audible. 'Picks—men breaking ground—excavatin' near the sewer . . .' He fainted again.

'Hang it, he's right,' exclaimed Rimmer. 'Some damned

fool has disregarded the embargo on building over sewers. That's what set the rats on the rampage. God knows where they are now and what havòc they have wrought.'

The homeless of London, we learned later, were at that moment sharing a little of the divine omniscience. The rats had made for the central bridges of the Thames, Westminster, Charing Cross, and Blackfriars; there they had swarmed upon the paupers who sought shelter under the mighty spans, circles of men and women squatting around fires of driftwood, boiling stews of soiled vegetables and putrified meat, passing from hand to hand bottles of gin or a caustic substitute to keep out the bite of the wind that whooped under the arches and sprinkled them with snow. The coming of the rats was sudden and their victims were too weak, too drunk or too numbed with cold to resist them. Frail bodies fell, each to be pinioned by twoscore muscular brutes; arms and heels flailed briefly then lay limp; cauldrons rolled from their tripods and spilled their greasy contents over man and rat alike; and cinders flew as sprawling limbs were dragged across burning embers. At Westminster and Charing Cross the toll of death was high, the damage to the bridges light; but at Blackfriars a cinder must have lodged upon the wooden auxiliary bridge, fallen upon a stack of planking, or caught in a tarry joint. Old bridge and new smouldered, burned, blazed. The flames were whipped by the wind towards the wharves and ware-houses farther east. The river front was soon engulfed in the worst conflagration since the Tooley Street fire and, before that, the Great Fire itself.

It was not only the waterfront that burned: the river itself was on fire. Schooners and lighters crammed with oil, tar, and tallow, made frenzied efforts to put out from their wharves into the middle of the stream, but the tugs that tried to tow them collided and left them to drift helplessly. Burning cargoes, hastily jettisoned, were whirled into collision by the currents and, coalescing, formed a solid phalanx of flaming wood, which hung in mid-stream until the wind took it and sent it spinning towards the shipping in the docks farther to the east. The port was saved from total destruction by the sturdy floating engines of the Metropolitan Fire Brigade. Cumbersome vessels, they were, little more than great platforms from which pumps could be operated; but their captains were river-men, nonetheless, who knew every swirl of a current and every manoeuvre of which their hulks were capable. Seeing the hazard of the floating wreckage, a flotilla of them drew away from the river front and set off in pursuit of it. With the aid of a trio of steam tugs, which were risked countless times by their skippers in cutting-out expeditions that Nelson would have cheered, the engines broke up the mass and played their hoses on the burning cargoes, ships, and pieces of ships that composed it, until the danger was past.

No sooner had that threat receded, however, than another replaced it. In the path of the fire lay a warehouse, stuffed with cotton by a merchant while prices soared during the scarcity that had emptied the mills of Lancashire. The superintendent of the metropolitan brigade wanted to tear it down and dump its precious contents in the river, but the owner forestalled him, pleading that the building be allowed to take its chance; his entire fortune, he wept, was baled within it. The superintendent threw back his head to bellow his orders to his captains, but his final decision was never revealed; a shed that adjoined the warehouse and contained, unknown to any but its absent owners, saltpetre and tar, exploded and took superintendent, merchant, and cotton with it.

All this we heard the following day, when smoke still hung above the river. That night, however, as we urged a churlish driver to take his cab at an easy pace across London to Shoreditch, we were concerned only with Scud, who lay across us in high fever. The crimson glare from the Thameside sky deepened the flush upon his face and the purple marks upon his neck. He threshed about him and raved—of the children without faces in the omnibus—of his little Bridie—of the war-lords in the sewers—of the heedless sojer—and of his friend Mr Rimmer; he even spoke of me and I wept as he muttered warnings to Matt—Matt with all that skill in his young fingers. The driver reined in. We were

120

at Scud's lodgings. Rimmer went ahead to prepare Mrs Scud and came back to help me with the body.

'Dear God,' breathed the little Irishwoman, when she saw the wound upon her husband's neck, ''twas a divil left a mark like that.'

'Dear God,' echoed Rimmer as we left, 'let him live. And if he does not, give me vengeance on his murderer.'

VIII
Profiteers

From Shoreditch we drove to Covent Garden, our cab-driver resigned to the fact that it was going to be a long, cold night. Rimmer ordered him to thread the streets that followed the line of the sewer until we reached the point where, according to his reckoning, the noise of excavation had originated. It lay, we found, in the parish of St Giles. There was no sign of demolition or rebuilding on the main thoroughfare, but the tenements which lined it on one side were strangely uncurtained and unlit; on entering an alley that led to their rear, we discovered that they were merely shells, a façade to conceal from the inquisitive an extensive site on which men laboured by the light of shrouded torches, some demolishing existing houses, others digging foundations for new. Whoever owned and worked the site was making rapid progress that he did not want to publicize.

A figure rose out of the darkness and barred our way. I remembered having engraved Hackett's reconstruction of Neanderthal man and decided that this had been his model. A retreating brow, splayed nose, and negroid lips were matched by arms that dangled to the knees and a torso like a palaeozoic crag. He swung a pick in his left hand as if it were no heavier than a hammer, and his manner lacked warmth; this may have been attributable to the toshers' garb that we wore and that was hardly suitable for leaving cards; but had we appeared in coronets and ermine, I doubt if our reception would have been more gracious.

'Orff,' said Neanderthal Man. 'Orff!'

Evidently one who dispensed with the customary formalities of conversation. But Rimmer could be equally terse. 'Your employer,' he snapped. 'Now.'

122

Neanderthal Man felt happiest with proven formulae. 'Orff,' he repeated. Then, when he saw that it had no effect, he revealed a vocabulary of unexpected dimensions. 'Aht,' he said. 'Aht.'

'Your employer is breaking the law,' Rimmer explained. 'I want to see him.'

Neanderthal Man's last efflorescence had clearly exhausted his repertoire, so he tried to smash Rimmer's skull instead. He would have succeeded, had Rimmer not been anticipating him and caught his wrist in a grip acquired from a Chinese pirate—'Retired, reformed and working as a Baptist missionary, capital fellow'—which forced him to release his weapon. Further conversation seemed bootless and we retired under Neanderthal Man's brooding eye, an eye that promised bloody revenge.

Rimmer told our driver to take us to Little Newport Street, where we put on clean clothes, and thence to Durston's office. Durston had left and we were directed to his club, the Euclid, an exclusive retreat for mathematicians, where we missed him again and were given his home address. We repeated it to our driver, who remarked in bitter reproach that he hoped as how we'd visit him when he was flat on his back with the pneumonics and maybe say a prayer for him when he was gone to drive a hansom in the sky.

Durston lived in new and stylish mansions at Queen's Gate. He opened the door himself and allowed a fractional quiver of the eyebrow to express his surprise at our unheralded arrival; he made no reference to it, however, as he ushered us into his study and unstoppered some capital port. While Rimmer explained the reason for our visit, I looked about me. The unusual combination of the elegant and the *outré* that had characterized Durston's office, was repeated on a grander scale in his residence. Three walls were devoted to the Pre-Raphaelites: two stunning Rossettis were flanked by a sketch for *The Light of the World* and a superb Millais; there were some drawings in an unfamiliar style that I now attribute to the young Burne-Jones, and one of the better Collinsons. The fourth wall was devoted to original medievalia: an altarpiece of the Quattrocento, a Pisan

Madonna, and a Crucifixion by one of the Flemish masters. One corner of the room held a piece by Woolner, another a Morris chair. The bookcases warped under the works of the Rossettis, Ruskin, Stephens, and Morris. A dozen illuminated manuscripts and incunables lay face upwards on shelves and lecterns. Rimmer finished as I completed my inventory, and Durston sat, eyes upon his glass, in meditation.

'I should not have thought that there is much that we can do,' he murmured. 'There are bound to be infractions of our orders and we cannot devote our limited resources to punishing every single one.'

Remembering his attitude to Maginn, I was puzzled by his reply and Rimmer was frankly disgusted. 'That infraction, as you call it, may have cost Scud his life. Tom Scud, the only one amongst us with a wife and family to care for. In any case, the secrecy and speed with which the site in St Giles is being developed make me think that its owner has some illegality to conceal.'

Durston's face and tone were expressionless. 'I regret there is nothing more that I can do.' His voice shook a little. 'I—I—respected Mr Scud.'

We left, dispatched an express to Hammersmith, telling McWhirrie and Gunn of Scud's plight, and went home; but not to bed, for neither of us felt like sleep. Instead, we stoked up the fire, brewed mugs of tea, and checked references to metacarpals until St Anne's clock chimed one. I rose and peered out at the dark streets, in time to catch a movement in the doorway opposite. I called softly to Rimmer to snuff the candles and, having done so, he joined me at the window.

'Doorway of number 37,' I muttered. 'Someone's watching.'

'Too small,' mused Rimmer, 'for a constable. I suppose you haven't by any chance acquired a female admirer. If so, you can pack your bags. I've managed to avoid them myself, and I don't intend to be bothered with yours.'

I denied the suggestion indignantly and Rimmer, relieved, outlined a modest outflanking operation via the lower back window. We departed by the means suggested and took a circuitous route through an alley to come upon number 37 from both sides. There was a scuffle, and I found myself putting an arm-lock, as taught to Rimmer by an Indian thug—'uncommonly good-natured for a fellow with sixty murders to his credit'—on the spindly limb of Dicky Pitts.

''Ere,' he squeaked, 'wossa gime?'

Just what we had intended to ask, I informed him, and we marched him off to our rooms. Our assumptions, he insisted, were wrong. He had not been casing the crib for a burglary; he had—a long pause while his eyes flickered around him—he had simply wanted to pass on some information to us, had chosen a late hour to escape detection, and had hesitated at the last minute, in order to have it out with his conscience, which was upbraiding him.

'Nivver peached on no one afore,' he exclaimed, after his long and involved monologue, 'an' it comes 'ard at fust.'

On whom, asked Rimmer, did he intend to inform?

'Why, on ol' Tommy Dalton, Mr Enthony Norris as now is. Cove you was arskin' abaht.'

'Well?' Rimmer, I could see, was not impressed by Dicky's generous notion, which sounded suspiciously like a spur-of-the-minute alibi; nor, for that matter was I, although I could not help admiring the little villain's impudence.

'I 'ev 'eard,' Dicky assumed the portentous manner of a constable in a witness box, 'I 'ev 'eard as 'ow Mr Enthony Norris, hesquire, 'es summink on the go what is not only illegal but dahnright criminal.'

'In what way?' I asked.

'I ain't a man as meddles much in politics,' Dicky abandoned the constable and became an expansive philosopher, 'live an' let live bein' my motter; but I takes it 'ard when a men like Mr Enthony turns agin' 'is own clarss and drives 'em 'omeless inter the street by takin' advantage o' their fears an' o' their lack o' learnin'.'

Rimmer dug out his watch. 'To what,' he asked with elaborate exasperation, 'is all this leading?'

'Why, to the fect that Enthony there is a-buyin' up 'ouses all over the plice, dirt cheap, cash on the nile, families an' lodgers aht the sime day; and 'ee's tearin' 'em dahn to rebuild 'em, fest es 'ee ken. Only when they're rebuilt, 'twon't be poor folks as 'ee'll be a-sellin' to, but yer gents from the City as needs a 'ouse nearby. An' you know 'ow it is 'ee ken get 'em so cheap?'

It may not have been intended as a question, but Rimmer answered it, nevertheless. 'Because of the rats. Norris is the man we've been hearing about, who's been snapping up property in St Giles and anywhere else where the rats have attacked in force. Am I right?'

'I should say so, guv'nor,' applauded Dicky.

I was puzzled. 'But we've tried to keep the menace of the rats a secret, sworn all sorts of people to silence, and muzzled the Press. How does Norris know in which areas the rats are causing trouble?'

'Someone on your side's 'elpin' 'im, ain't 'ee?' Dicky explained with exaggerated clarity. 'Up to you to find aht 'oo. I've discharged me dooty to the workin'-man, so I'll be orff.'

Rimmer showed him out; when he returned, I asked, 'Do you really think that was his reason for coming. Or did he invent it all when we caught him reconnoitring the house?'

'Don't know,' Rimmer replied. 'But lock up the valuables—such valuables as we possess, anyhow—just in case.'

We were, alas, bolting the stable door: Rimmer's watch-pocket was already empty.

I did not want to believe Pitts. If what he had told us was true, we had no need to search for Norris's informant. I myself had caught him *in flagrante delicto* in the Cut. But the next day, Sunday, a note from Pride and Passion, delivered by the disinfected hand of a mission urchin, brought corroboration. She enclosed a bill of sale for a house near the mission, which one of her patients had shown her. In it, Joseph Moody, cooper, of the first part, had bargained and sold his brick messuage in Maladroit Court to Thomas Dalton, builder, of the second part, for what was, even to my inexperienced eye, a trifling sum. The 'brick messuage' was a flea-ridden hovel that housed four other families besides Moody's. They were now seeking shelter together with Moody himself, since he had blown the entire purchase price

126

on liquor in one evening.

'Tommy Dalton,' sighed Rimmer. 'Norris's original name. Now he's using it as an alias to conceal his part in the transaction. Doubtless he has a solicitor in one pocket and a clerk from the Deeds Registry in another, to square the legal side, so that there is no way in which the whole nefarious business can be traced to that respectable gent, Anthony Norris, so highly thought of by the Lord Mayor and the Duchess of Aston. Humbug!'

This confirmation of Norris's guilt irredeemably inculpated Durston. My misery must have been apparent, for Rimmer, not normally a tender man, put aside Pride and Passion's letter and sat beside me.

'Matt,' he said, 'try to accustom yourself to the fact that human beings are not only ugly brutes, as I once told Miss Tiptree; they are also miserably weak. There are no good people: merely some who are less bad than others. Behind his arrogance, his languor and his cynicism, Durston is as vulnerable to temptation as you or I. In fact, he is more susceptible; for unlike us, he is burdened by a desire to possess beautiful things—paintings, sculpture and books. He doesn't go to swag shops for his clothes as we do, nor does he hunt for bargains on the City Road bookstalls. You've seen his office and his rooms; you know enough about art and decoration to realize that they were not furnished and adorned on a civil servant's salary alone. Even if his Rossettis and Millais were bought before their market value rose, those altarpieces and incunables must have cost hundreds. I should imagine that Durston has lived for some years far beyond his means, and that his complicity with Norris is an attempt to save himself from financial ruin.'

None of that need be true, I argued. Perhaps Durston had private means; perhaps I had made a mistake in the Cut and had not seen him at all; perhaps I had seen him, but his meeting with Norris had been coincidental, merely an enquiry for directions or the time, which Durston had subsequently forgotten. But each 'perhaps' sounded weaker than the last, and I stopped. Durston, I knew, was guilty. So, with the total irrationality of the disillusioned, I changed sides and began to vilify him. I poured scorn on all that I had admired: his cool elegance, his sophistication, his Olympian arrogance. He had betrayed me and I spared him nothing. Rimmer heard me out and, bless him, understood. Instead of damning me for a mindless oaf—his usual reaction to my fits of childishness—he filled his pipe and spoke quietly.

'Look, Matt, Durston may not be wholly at fault. Norris may have learned of his financial difficulties, if they existed, and have exerted pressure upon him to co-operate in the plot. Whatever the circumstances of his collusion, don't think that it would have been easy for him. We all engage in some sort of deception at some time in our lives, but it's a deuced heavy burden to carry for long.'

Unconsciously, he had echoed Durston's own words, the spoken thought: 'to awake each morning and take up the same heavy burden . . .' and I understood.

I waited, then asked what we should do.

'See Yelverton. There's no other way, I'm afraid. If this were a novelette, we'd turn in Norris and let Durston do the decent thing with a rope or a revolver. But we're in the brutal reality of the nineteenth century and two men are profiting in the middle of a war at the expense of poor and frightened people. So be damned to the novelette. I intend to expose them.' His voice hardened. 'Moreover, Norris's greed may have killed Scud, and Durston would have shielded him. I'm a pretty good hater, Matt, and I can't forgive that.'

We saw Yelverton on Monday: we laid siege to his outer walls, inner walls, curtain walls, and bastions of clerks; we took panelled door after panelled door, overran office after office, and demolished a portcullis of frowns and sneers; with the result that at noon we were shown into the Under-secretary's chambers. On his desk lay a pile of notes sent in advance of our coming by the functionaries that we had vanquished.

'You state that your business is of the most urgent and confidential nature,' said the plum, fingering the pile. 'Very well, you have three minutes in which to make good your assertion.'

Rimmer needed only one. 'Mr Ashley Durston, an official

of your department, who has been closely concerned with the eradication of rats from the sewers, has taken advantage of his position to assist a speculative builder, named Thomas Dalton, alias Anthony Norris, in buying property at unfair prices from people who have been terrified by the incursions of the rats. Norris is tearing down this property and rebuilding quickly, so that when the menace of the rats has abated, he can sell off his new houses at a high profit, before anyone can question the morality or legality of his methods.'

'Your proof,' demanded Yelverton.

Rimmer supplied it.

Yelverton heard him out, then spoke with ill-suppressed violence. 'The statements of two youths, one of them an escaped convict whom you appear to have abetted illegally, the other your own protégé, who has, in my opinion, for too long been privy to matters beyond his concern and, as your allegations suggest, his understanding.' His voice rose. 'I resent the slur cast upon one of my most able administrators. And I deplore your calumny against Mr Norris. He is a member of my club and we are not in the custom of admitting scoundrels to our smoking-room.' He regained control of himself. 'I intend to dismiss you, Mr Rimmer, without further action. But I warn you, should these charges be repeated, in any circumstances, I shall see that you suffer the full rigour of the law. Good day.'

'Do we drop it?' I asked, as we walked across Whitehall.

'Damned if we do,' said Rimmer and took me to eat mutton pies at a stall in Scotland Yard.

It was in the middle of a mouthful of rubbery meat, heavily spiced to disguise its age, that Rimmer had an inspiration and shouted, 'Lemon!' Explaining to the bewildered stallkeeper, who produced one, that he had meant something else, Rimmer hurried me off to Fleet Street. We stopped at number 85, the offices of *Punch*. Rimmer asked for the editor, Mark Lemon, but was told that he and his staff were lunching in Bedford Street, off the Strand. We turned about and marched to the Bedford Hotel, where we discovered Lemon at the head of a table, leading his colleagues in a comic song. Rimmer received a boisterous greeting and the offer of 'claret or porter or brandy-and-water', before Lemon perceived his sober demeanour, excused himself to the company, and ushered us into an anteroom.

'My dear fellow,' he said to Rimmer, 'you're not in debt, are you? Sick? Married?'

'Nothing so dire,' Rimmer replied. 'I'm suffering from a bout of morality; and I need Mr Punch's help.'

He told Lemon as much of the truth as he dared: that a civil servant was making use of privileged information to assist a speculative builder in the slums, but that he lacked proof with which to satisfy the authorities.

'Then I thought of *Punch*. I want to drive them into the open with some sort of message that we are on to them, and that message could be in the form of a drawing, referring to their collusion.'

Lemon took the point, but explained that moral judgements were not in *Punch*'s line; there were periodicals of a crusading sort, however, and others that thrived upon scandal; surely these would be of more assistance? No moral judgements, laughed Rimmer: what of Hood's 'Song of the Shirt' and Lemon's own 'Pauper's Christmas Carol'? As for the yellow press, it might help, but not at once. The cartoon must appear immediately, and *Punch* was the only magazine with which he had any influence. As an occasional contributor, and as a friend, he begged Lemon to help.

'We'll put it to the vote,' said Lemon and led us back to the dining-room.

Interrupting a glee, Lemon explained our predicament, our proposal, and, with a sidelong smile, his own sympathy to it. If Mr Punch was to be involved, however, he felt that the staff should be consulted first.

'I'm for it,' said Shirley Brooks at once. 'We've just time to revise a page of the next issue before Bradbury and Evans start to print.'

Henry Silver nodded agreement but reminded us that the engravers would be uncommon busy.

'Never mind,' said John Leech, 'I've an idea of my own about that.' '

Du Maurier was all for it but admitted that it was not his sort of subject; another recent recruit, Burnand, said it was just the topic for Tenniel.

'Away in the country,' sighed Lemon. 'What about it, Carlo?'

He looked towards Charles Keene, the principal artist present and, I knew, an arch-Tory. I had been watching him carefully and had guessed from his discouraging expression what his answer would be.

'I'm against the ploy on principle,' he declared, 'and should prefer to take no part in it.' It was as I had expected. 'Nevertheless,' he continued, and I looked up at the warmth in his tone, 'old Rimmer there has given me some capital ideas in the past, so I'll not fail him now. What d'ye propose for the contents?'

We were desperately short of time. Keene went off to improvise a studio in the smoking-room, while the rest of the table devised the picture and the legend. Within twenty minutes, Keene was at work. An hour later, we beheld the spires and towers of London, shrinking in terror from the looming shadow of Pests and Pestilence, while from the rear of the city two figures skipped with bulging money-bags, initialled A.D. and A.N., past blindfolded policemen and judges. The caption, Lemon's own suggestion, was brief: 'The Law and the Profiteers'. Lemon said that he would take it directly to the engravers, and we prepared to leave with him, but Leech caught us at the door.

'Take it to Dalziel,' he urged. 'I'll come, too. I've still a little pull there.'

How great his 'pull' was, we discovered when, on arriving at Dalziel's, we were told by the engraver that all his crafts-men were engaged and that he could not deal with our commission. Leech asked if there was a free bench; several, owing to sickness, admitted the engraver.

'Then we have someone to fill it,' said Leech, and pushed me forward. A silence followed, broken only by the trip-hammer which had replaced my heart. Lemon said at last that it was alright by him, as long as Leech knew what he was about. The engraver was perplexed but agreed that if Mr

Leech would vouch for the lad, why, he would give him all he needed.

'Certainly, I'll vouch for Mathew,' Leech affirmed. 'I know his work, both as artist and engraver, and I'd happily entrust my own drawings to his knife.'

All of which was very flattering, no doubt, but made my hand precious unsteady when, at last, I was seated at a bench with boxwood and tools before me. Fortunately, Keene had been sparing with his lines—he had had no alternative in the time allotted to him—and the re-drawing and engraving took less time and trouble than I had been accustomed to devote to the offences against Nature committed by little Lampiner and Hackett. Dalziel inspected the completed block and nodded approval; Leech examined it and smiled his praise; and Lemon clapped my shoulder and told me I was a trump. Rimmer stood aside, meanwhile, wearing the smile of a lion whose cub has just brought home its first Sunday dinner. The block was parcelled and dispatched to the printer's, with a screed of instructions for the alteration of page 2, and Lemon carried us back to Fleet Street for a drink. His staff found excuses to slip into the office to ask how the engraving had gone and to share the festive brandy that Lemon had produced.

'The criminals,' commented Brooks, with a nod to Lemon and myself, 'are now *marked* men.'

It was six o'clock when we returned to Little Newport Street. McWhirrie and Gunn stood there, the one hailing a cab, the other pinning a note to our door. They explained that they had been waiting for us as usual, when a message had come from Miss Tiptree, urging us to join her at Scud's home in Shoreditch. They had decided to wait no longer, since Miss Tiptree's messages inevitably presaged some sort of disaster. We took two cabs, paid the drivers double to race across icy London and, arriving at Scud's house, hurried up to his rooms. Pride and Passion awaited us; having come, she said, to help Mrs Scud, she had been shocked at the deterioration in Scud's condition.

'Mrs Scud has done all that could be done,' she added. 'No hospital could have achieved more. But the poison has coursed through his body faster than any remedy devised by Nature or Man.'

We entered the bedroom where Scud lay. Mrs Scud sat beside the bed, cooling the shrivelled face upon the pillow. She rose and left us alone with her husband, suppressing her sobs until she was beyond hearing. Scud stared up at us and twisted his lips into a grin.

'He can't talk,' whispered Pride and Passion, 'but he can understand all you say.'

Rimmer bent over the Irishman and pressed his hand.

'Listen, old chap,' he said, 'your wife, your children will all be well cared for, you have my word.'

Scud's eyes showed gratitude.

'If you have any dependants in Ireland,' Rimmer went on, 'we shall make provision for them also.'

The eyes thanked him again.

Rimmer tried a jovial tone. 'We haven't done for the rats yet, but we shall; and when we do, your part won't go unmarked.'

It was an error. Be damned tew that, the eyes said. Will glory help me now?

'Ach,' McWhirrie muttered to me in despair, 'fit can ye say or dee? I canna bear a death-bed.'

He had spoken more audibly than he knew, and the twisted grin grew broader. If yees faind it hard, the eyes said, what d'yees think it's laike for me?

Mrs Scud slipped back among us; with her was a priest. Then I heard a voice, Gunn's voice, no longer pompous but gentle and meditative.

'I knew your part of Ireland, Scud. Went there once to see an ancient monastic cell. Did I ever tell you?'

The eyes sought his.

'One evening, I remember, they took me out in a little trap, along a white road that slid in and out of the hills, until it stopped abruptly. I descended and found that I was on a cliff; and there, beyond, was the Atlantic.'

The eyes rested upon him.

'The waves were rolling in like thunder on the shore and the spray was hanging in the air, mingled with a warm drizzle of rain. I sat on the turf and smoked; and the gulls swooped down on me for trespassing.'

The twisted grin softened to a reminiscent smile.

'Just then, I heard a piping. I thought it was a sea-bird, but when I looked behind me, in a field two children were dancing to a penny whistle . . .'

The rattle in the throat was soft, so soft that it was some seconds before we saw that Scud was dead.

When we left, McWhirrie and Gunn preceded us to the cabs. For a moment, the old professor rested his hand upon his companion's arm; then they mounted and were driven off.

Rimmer had arranged for a copy of the amended *Punch* to be delivered by hand to Durston as soon as it had left the press. There was, therefore, nothing for us to do when we rose, but wait to see if Rimmer's plan would succeed. After breakfast Rimmer bent over his desk, writing memoranda to Yelverton, Owen, and the Board of Works, informing them of Scud's death and proposing that provision should be made for his family. I turned the leaves of my sketch-books and looked at my drawings of the little Irishman, from the day we had met him on the embankment at Westminster until our last descent into the sewers. I was beginning a final sketch, the wasted face upon the pillow, as I remembered it, when St Anne's clock struck ten and an inspector of police came to the door. His name, he said, was Preece; and his accent enabled Rimmer, who prided himself upon his ear, to assign him, correctly, to Pembrokeshire. He explained that Lord Yelverton had sent him, having received a letter from a Mr Ashley Durston of the Home Department, with an enclosure addressed to us. Rimmer opened the envelope that the inspector proffered and read its contents aloud.

Gentlemen,

A peccant servant of the public applauds your persistence and congratulates you upon your success. I have nothing to say in my defence, save that my excesses were committed in galleries and not at gaming-tables, and that I was from the beginning in Norris's power—extortionate usury and blackmail are two of his principal sources of influence. An expensive advocate might make something of both points at the Old Bailey, but I have no intention of providing him with the opportunity. Like a punctilious official and a good general, I have kept an open line of retreat; and by the time this comes to hand, I shall be well on my way beyond the jurisdiction of the courts.

I remain your far from humble, and regrettably disobedient, but, I trust, generally civil, servant,

Ashley Durston

'Arrogant to the end,' murmured Rimmer. 'I wonder where he's gone.'

'Italy, I shouldn't wonder, sir,' said Inspector Preece; adding, in answer to Rimmer's questioning eyepatch, 'I took note of his artistic predilections when ordered to search his apartments.' He reflected. 'Good stuff, some of it; but not a patch on Turner. Begging your pardon, sir.'

Rimmer provided bread, cheese, and beer, and asked about Norris.

'I was sent to arrest him, sir, since Mr Durston's letter to Lord Yelverton provided enough evidence of legal chicanery and of his past activities to send him away for twenty years. But he wasn't at home nor yet at his place of business.'

'What about his club?' I asked.

'Nor there, lad. Lord Yelverton carried out the search himself, discreetly, to spare the members' feelings.'

'That leaves his building sites,' said Rimmer. 'Let's try the one we know of, in St Giles. We'll show you the way, Preece.'

Our passage through the parish was halted when our cab joined a long queue of stationary traffic, near Pride and Passion's mission. We dismounted, and went by foot the rest of the way to the building site. As we passed the head of the queue, we saw that the impediment was a monstrous traction-engine, which smoked and rumbled across the cobbles, towing a machine for all the world like some medieval engine of war. It consisted of two massive, conical rollers, studded with spikes and mounted on angled axles, elevated a few inches from the ground by a pair of running wheels. It was, Preece told us, a road-breaker.

'Bound for Norris's site?' wondered Rimmer, as we struck

135

through a tangle of alleys to avoid the crowds that lined the streets to view the novelty.

When we arrived at the site we saw the barrel-like Norris at once; he stood in the centre of a stretch of cleared ground, conferring with Neanderthal Man. The latter recognized us and alerted his employer to our identities, but Norris suffered us to approach, his manner effusive.

'About the other evening, is it, gentlemen? Awfully sorry. Fact is, my foreman here is a trifle over-zealous. Kept the men at work all night. Clean forgot about the circular. I've given him a piece of my mind, I can tell you, and I assure you it won't happen again. Now you've come a long way,' he reached into his pocket, 'perhaps a little refreshment . . .'

Inspector Preece allowed the flurry of words to subside. Then: 'Am I addressing Mr Norris or Mr Dalton, sir? Mr Durston did not make it clear which name you went under when on the site.'

Preece had intended to stun Norris with this gambit and to put the cuffs on him while he groped for a reply. But he had reckoned without Neanderthal Man, who, at the mention of Durston's name, displayed a mental celerity of which I would not have thought him capable; he locked a simian arm around Preece's neck, buckled Rimmer's knees with a sweeping kick, and bellowed to Norris to run. I pursued the fat man, but his well-muscled calves took him across the cleared ground and into the cover of half-demolished tenements that formed the far border of the site. By the time I had reached them, he was scaling their outer wall and I realized that he could drop thence into the streets of St Giles and escape in the cover of the throng. As I followed him up the wall, he pulled himself on to a girder that marked the level of the second storey, inserted himself through the remains of a window and stood poised there, one hand grasping the embrasure, steadying himself to jump. Just then, something small and brown scuttered along the beam behind him and ran across his hand. A rat. I saw the hand snatched in horror from the window-frame, watched as it threshed the air, and heard Norris scream as he lost his balance and fell. I reached another window and looked down. Norris was on the cobbles, both legs, from their distorted angle, broken, trying to pull himself out of the way of the traction engine, which was almost upon him. The driver wrenched at the steering-handle; sparks flew from the wheels as he tried to reverse their motion; but the engine did not stop. Ten tons of metal rolled over Norris's body and the spikes on the road-breaker tore to shreds the pulpy mass beneath.

At noon we met Yelverton and Crashaw at the Rifles' barracks. Pride and Passion joined us, and the committee was complete when Owen and Bazalgette arrived, bringing with them, to our surprise, McWhirrie and Gunn. Yelverton rose and made a speech. First, he lamented the loss of Scud, 'a man of courage and devotion to duty, who may fairly be said to have laid down his life in our cause'; any representations concerning his dependants would be heard sympathetically by the Home Department. Next, he turned to another matter for grief, grief of a different nature. A member of his staff, a trusted and respected member, had committed a sin unforgivable in a public servant, the misuse of privileged information. Yelverton looked at Rimmer.

'I am bound to say,' he declared, 'that when suspicion first fell upon Mr Durston and his associate, I heedlessly repudiated it. I wish to apologize now to Mr Rimmer for my response to his original allegations.'

Lastly, said the chairman, there was the problem of the rats. Here, however, he was pleased to announce that a solution had been found. Colonel Crashaw had spent the last three days in consultation with the most eminent toxicologists in the country—but, he smiled, he would let the colonel speak for himself. Crashaw rose, took a phial from his pocket, and scattered crystals from it upon the table before him.

'Poison,' he stated, 'poison of the most deadly nature when mixed with water. Poison that will rid us of the rats in hours. I propose to send my own men, men of the Queen's Royal Rifles, into the sewers, armed with paper capsules containing the crystals, which they will fire from specially-adapted rifles—I am having the modifications made at this minute—into every drain, every gully, every crevice in the entire sewer system. It will be the most comprehensive exercise of its kind ever mounted; and it will succeed. You may rest assured of that.'

He resumed his seat, the meagre whiskers at his chin almost erect with exultation. Into the silence that followed, Pride and Passion spoke in tones of incredulity.

'Have you thought of the danger?'

'Of course,' snapped Crashaw. 'I am assured that it is trifling. The poison produces no effluvium and is rapidly dispersed; moreover, Mr Bazalgette's exertions over the past years have ensured that our water supply runs no risk of contamination.'

'And what of the rookeries, the slums, where open sewers and cesspools still abound, despite Mr Bazalgette's reforms; where children paddle in gutters and sewage continually bubbles back from choked drains? Discharge your poison, Colonel Crashaw, and in twenty-four hours you will have put hundreds, nay, thousands of lives at risk.'

'Miss Tiptree is right,' Rimmer said with deliberation. 'Enough lives have been wasted; there is no need to compound the folly.'

'Bazalgette and I agree,' Owen came to his support. 'Lord Yelverton, you cannot let this scheme go forward.'

Yelverton's eyes circled the table; his pomposity was gone; he was an elderly, tired, and stupid man, faced with a problem that he had neither the wit nor character to resolve.

'Have I any alternative?' he asked.

IX
The last campaign

'Aye,' said McWhirrie, 'ye have. That's the reason I'm here.'

He removed from his pocket a crumpled sheet of foolscap and smoothed it.

'Noo, this is nae a' o' ma ain devisin', ye ken. Me an' Gunn hae bin rackin' oor brains owre it, file Rimmer an' Matt hae bin stravagin' alang the sewers. Then Owen, tae, an' Maister Bazalgette, they've gie'en a haun' wi' the details.'

He began to read points from his paper. *Primo*, he asked, what means of destroying the rats were open to us? Shooting? Had been tried and failed. Flushing? Tried and failed, too. Trapping? Had not been given a proper trial but was impractical, anyway, on the scale we were envisaging. Poison? This with a glare at Crashaw. Not to be considered. No, the only sure means of extermination revealed by our recent adventures was . . . fire.

'You surely do not intend to risk a subterranean conflagration?' Crashaw's tone was of outrage. 'And you accuse me of endangering the populace!'

'Wheesht,' McWhirrie silenced him.

Secundo, we had tried hitherto to fight the rats on their own territory, in the sewers. Was there any reason, however, why we should not choose a battlefield to suit ourselves?

'If you ask them nicely,' sneered Crashaw, 'they might even form ranks on Aldershot parade-ground and salute as you kill them.'

McWhirrie found it beneath his dignity to reply. The corollary of his *primo* and *secundo*, he asserted, was *tertio*: if the rats could be driven to a site chosen by us, there to be

139

destroyed by fire, how could our weapon be used against them? Simply, by driving them into a trap prepared with explosive and detonating it.

'First asking them to sit quietly while you light the fuses,' Crashaw scoffed.

McWhirrie continued to ignore him. *Quarto*, where was there an area near London large enough to contain an explosion of great force? The answer had been provided by Owen: Barking Marsh. *Quinto*, how were the rats to be transported there? Bazalgette had solved this one: by driving them through the Middle and High Level intercepting sewers.

'If Colonel Crashaw was unable to dislodge a few rats from the Covent Garden sewer,' asked Yelverton, who had displayed increasing interest as McWhirrie had progressed, and a corresponding impatience with Crashaw's interruptions, 'how can you hope to drive rats from all the sewers into the intercepting channels?'

McWhirrie pointed to the blue spiral above Rimmer's head. 'Smoke,' he said.

'I refuse to listen to any more of this twaddle,' snapped Crashaw. 'Do you propose to enroll the populations of the smoking-rooms of London to blow smoke rings down every manhole?'

'Your facetiousness ill becomes your rank, Colonel Crashaw.' Yelverton spoke quietly but the menace of his tone was unmistakeable.

'The simple smoke ball, as in service with the Royal Artillery, wull dee us jist fine.' McWhirrie was undisturbed. 'We'll leave the smokers in peace tae enjoy their baccy.' He addressed himself to Yelverton. 'Yon's oor plan in ootline, milord. Wull ye gie it yer support?'

Yelverton fingered his whiskers. 'Gentlemen, and Miss Tiptree,' he said, 'I have hitherto endorsed the Army's measures to deal with the problem of the rats. Both attempts have been dismal failures. Moreover, I have been guilty of misjudgement in a case of dishonesty within my own department. Mr Rimmer, in contrast, has consistently opposed the Army's plans; and it was his vigilance that uncovered the

140

peculation of my subordinate and terminated a monstrous attempt to profit from the fears of poor people. I propose to take his advice on the two schemes now before us. Mr Rimmer, which do you recommend?'

Rimmer's reply was succinct. He picked up Crashaw's crystals and tossed them upon the fire, where they burnt with a flame of jade. 'Safest place for those, what?' he said. 'Now, how do we use the smoke balls?'

Crashaw rose in fury. 'The Army's scheme having been so summarily rejected, the Army will take no further responsibility for the conduct of operations against the rats.'

'The Army will do as it is told,' said Yelverton. 'Sit down, Crashaw, there's a good fellow, and don't sulk.'

Rimmer's question was answered by Owen. They suggested, he said, a mass invasion of the sewers by Riflemen and Artillerymen, who would fire balls, cartridges and canisters of smoke into every drain, gully and branch of each sewer; if possible, they would use fuses to delay the action of the missiles; where this proved impractical, they would issue the men with a primitive mask of charcoal and gauze, sufficient to protect them until they left through their prescribed manholes.

Pride and Passion leaned forward. How would they prepare the public for the sudden appearance of smoke and fumes from manholes and gratings, she asked. Advertisements and announcements, replied Bazalgette; a new method of fumigation undergoing tests, something like that.

Rimmer had more questions. How was the trap with the explosives to be prepared? How was the explosive to be detonated simultaneously over such a large area? Owen took the first: it had been recently asserted by a London inventor that gunpowder could be rendered inactive and protected from damp by the addition of finely-ground glass powder, which could be extracted quickly by sieving. Simultaneous detonation, explained Bazalgette, fielding the second, could be achieved by an electrical circuit recently developed by the Royal Artillery Institution. McWhirrie coughed: he felt impelled to add, he said, that both techniques were still at an experimental stage and had never been considered for use on the scale we envisaged; nevertheless, the essay, he believed, was worth making.

From questions, Rimmer turned to suggestions. 'In order to give your smoke bombers a fair chance in the sewers, why shouldn't we do as every great general does and create a diversion?'

'Where?' asked Yelverton.

'Along the Metropolitan Line,' Rimmer answered, 'which the rats already hold and will consequently rally to defend.'

'A sound scheme,' approved Bazalgette, 'but how do you propose to launch your attack? The rats have done considerable damage to the company's rolling stock, although the line may still be intact. And how would you protect your men?'

Rimmer was silenced. I was not. 'Er . . .' I said and repeated it several times before anyone paid attention. 'Er, last year I engraved some pictures of American ships.'

'Is this relevant, Matt?' Rimmer asked, seeing that a scowl was empurpling Yelverton's face.

'Truly,' I assured him. 'They were steam frigates, totally encased in armour-plating, fighting along the Mississippi. Well . . .' I began to falter as the committee regarded me blankly, 'well—couldn't we construct an iron-clad train?'

No one replied. I could have howled with humiliation.

Bazalgette laughed softly. 'Damned if the lad hasn't hit on the answer. Iron plating, embrasures for the Riflemen to fire from, complete protection for the engineers. Capital!'

The committee applauded. I glowed.

Gunn spoke. 'To one elaboration of the scheme, may I add another? Might we not add to the effect of our diversion by a surprise attack upon the Hungerford warren, the war-lords' domain?'

'We've failed repeatedly to surprise them in the sewers,' commented Owen. 'They are ever alert.'

'I had not intended to suggest that the infiltration of the sewers was an essential constituent of my design,' Gunn replied.

'Then how . . .?'

'There is one subterranean thoroughfare, the capacities of

which have not been evaluated in our discussions hitherto,'
explained Gunn. 'I refer to the tube of the Pneumatic
Despatch Company.' The firm, he told us, existed to
transport parcels across London in cylinders operated by
atmospheric propulsion. The main tube for this purpose ran
from Holborn to the General Post Office; but there were
several experimental lines, one of which ran from
Westminster to Holborn, passing close enough to
Hungerford for us to disembark and force a way into the
warren.

'Man,' McWhirrie was scandalized. 'We're no' parcels.
Hoo can we mak' use o' yer tube?'

The cylinders, Gunn explained, were large enough to take
a man. Rimmer pressed him: was this hearsay, or did he
know for certain?

'I speak with some authority,' said Gunn, speaking with
some authority, 'since I have travelled in one myself.'

'You?' cried McWhirrie.

'I,' repeated Gunn. 'A trial run, no more.'

'Why?' asked McWhirrie, still unable to conceive of an
adventurous Gunn who volunteered to be sucked through the
earth in a vacuum.

'Because I was invited,' Gunn told him, adding modestly,
'I am one of the company's principal shareholders.'

Pride and Passion led our acclaim of Gunn's idea and
asked how we proposed to co-ordinate the campaign, so that
the trapping and extermination of the rats might be fully
effective.

'By telegraph,' Rimmer supposed.

Crashaw intervened. He had sat in sullen silence since
Yelverton's rebuke; but as the debate had continued, he had
followed it with mounting enthusiasm. He abandoned the
last vestiges of his pique to suggest, 'A balloon. Anchored
above the point at which the rats enter the trap, linked by
heliographic signals to each metropolitan operation. The
entire exercise can be conducted from the sky.'

Such unexpected resourcefulness went far to redeem
Crashaw in Yelverton's eyes; he reminded the colonel that
measures against the rats were still nominally the respon-

sibility of the Army, and asked him to resume command. Rimmer, marking the colonel's enthusiasm, and recognizing that we would require his authority to ensure that we had the complete co-operation of Army establishments, seconded the invitation. Crashaw, flushed with delight, agreed and set a limit of forty-eight hours on our preparations.

'We can't do it in the time,' declared Owen.

'We can,' Yelverton contradicted him, 'if I go directly to the Prime Minister and demand the full and immediate assistance of the Army and the Navy and of any civilian institutions of which we have need.'

Those ensuing two days were, I believe, the most hectic of my life; my sketch-books, crammed with drawings of factories, foundries, and laboratories, and my notebooks, filled with the statements and narratives of the rest of the committee, testify to the unending round of visits, inspections, experiments, and conferences that occupied us.

A begrimed page in my sketch-book records our visit to Hall's gunpowder factory at Plumstead to order, and arrange for the delivery of, our explosive. The drawings show a thousand barrels, each containing 100 lb of powder, ranged in the magazine; working-men shuffling in cloth slippers to avoid striking sparks with nailed boots; trucks on wheels of gun-metal, running along wooden rails fixed with copper nails, to reduce friction; strings of barges bringing saltpetre and brimstone; and the desolate waste of Plumstead Marsh stretching on either side. We watched while soldiers trundled our barrels on leather strips to the jetty, to be transshipped to Barking; we saw a sergeant dash a pipe from the hand of a thoughtless private; and we saw the fear on soldiers' faces as they boarded the sailing barges containing the powder, knowing that they were crossing the Thames on floating bombs. We argued with the foreman, the undermanager, and the managing director of the factory, all of whom dismissed our scheme for neutralizing the powder as unfeasible; what might work for one keg, they maintained, would not for a hundred; and when we left, we were more than half persuaded that they were right.

A statement from Gunn shows how they were proved

wrong. He attended the laboratory of the inventor, Linus Lucas. Outside, in a yard, a temporary stove of red-hot bricks contained a fierce fire in which a poker glowed; on a bench stood an array of bowls, each holding a mixture of explosive and glass-powder in varying proportions; with these, Lucas, in top hat and overall, began his demonstrations. He touched with a lighted taper the first bowl, which had the least amount of glass in it; the gunpowder exploded as soon as it ignited; the second and third, with larger quantities of glass, burned but did not explode; the fourth, containing Lucas's recommended mixture, neither burned nor exploded— indeed, it extinguished the taper. Linus Lucas was something of a showman, however; he rolled forward a keg of his mixture, seized the red-hot poker and thrust it deep into the keg's interior. Gunn looked for cover, but there was no explosion, merely a dull smouldering and a deal of smoke. The inventor brought forth another keg, this time saturated with water; he extracted the glass from it and plunged the poker in once more; there was a bang that brought a constable to the door with complaints of shattered windows.

There is a report of Owen's visit to Sydenham Hill, where Meredith Blake, the explorer, housed *Gloriana*, the dirigible balloon on which he had crossed the Irish Sea and sunk in the Firth of Forth. He vowed that she was at our disposal, provided that he was allowed to command her and was compensated for any damage she might suffer. Owen, as President of the British Association for the Advancement of Science, had in the past commissioned Blake to make observations at great altitudes, and was happy to agree. He was taken to admire *Gloriana*; she was at the time no more than a pile of folded gores, brightly painted, and a wicker car; but Blake, who was much given to statistics, asserted that when the fifty gores, each measuring 105 feet long by 44 inches at the centre, were inflated, their volume was 112,000 cubic feet. A detachment of Artillerymen, under a Captain Mossop, was subsequently sent to transport *Gloriana* to Barking. Owen and Blake watched, their anxiety modified by amusement, as a sergeant and a corporal were nearly strangled by her net, four gunners were almost smothered by

145

her silken bag, and the captain himself narrowly escaped bisection when the teams that drew the two gun carriages on which he was mounting the car, took fright and bolted.

Also in my notebook is McWhirrie's description of his trip to the Artillery Institution at Woolwich, where two professors of artillery produced a dozen paper shells, each of different weights and thicknesses, filled with a composition which, upon ignition, evolved thick, black smoke. They met his demands for rifle-sized cartridges and grenade-sized canisters with incredulity; then, revelling in the challenge, they set about constructing specimens. When McWhirrie had nodded approval, they dispatched specifications to the Arsenal and to the Royal Small Arms Factory at Enfield, where the entire labour force had been conscripted to modify the modifications that Crashaw had already demanded for his soldiers' rifles.

The most imposing scenes that I witnessed were those of the production of the iron-clad train. One page of my sketch-book is occupied by a visit to the Admiralty, where we met Captain Hazard, an engineer in the office of the Surveyor of the Navy, who had worked with Cowper Coles, the inventor of the shield-ships on which the American iron-clads were based. We were, said Hazard, in luck: the dockyard at Chatham had ordered a quantity of plating for the armour of its new steam frigates, and the Admiralty had agreed that we should draw upon it for the construction of our armoured train. We were joined by engineers from the Metropolitan Railway Company and pored over plans, sections, and elevations of their locomotives, marking on them anchor points, overlaps, fields of fire and areas of maximum trajectory.

From the Admiralty we went to the Canal Ironworks, Poplar, where Hazard showed us tons of cold blast pig-iron melting in cupolas. Screwing our eyes against the glare, the smoke and the gritty draughts which plagued the foundry workshops, we saw it scooped in ladles that hung from beams above us, and discharged into moulds, whence it was taken, hissing, to the slotting and planing machines to emerge in the form of plates four inches thick. Did we think, asked Hazard anxiously, that our men would feel safe behind them? We said that we thought they might. The plates were carried overhéad by cranes to the hydraulic ram, where they were bent and folded into the shapes required for the exterior of our train. In contrast to the din of the foundry, the ram worked almost silently; a single workman was at its controls, lowering each plate on to the cylinder of the press, locking it into place under weights, and bringing up the ram in the centre, to force the plate into the correct arc or angle. The plates were drawn by steam tractors to the sheds of the railway company at King's Cross, where they were welded to the body of the *Jupiter*, the locomotive selected for the assault, under Hazard's direction; while officers of the Rifles and the Artillery swarmed over the carriages, marking firing positions and preparing in the centre of each compartment ammunition dumps and loading points.

'Who has the honour of taking the *Jupiter* into action?' asked Hazard of a company director, who surveyed the scene with uncomprehending eyes.

'We've not yet found a volunteer,' the director admitted.

'You have now,' said Hazard.

A final leaf of my sketch-book portrays another scene of desolation. I made the sketches as I stood with Rimmer on Barking Marsh: sea-birds mewed overhead, the wind sang dolefully through the marsh grasses, and a thousand men supplied a dismal descant; they were navvies, rushed across from the drainage scheme for the south bank of the river, to excavate a trench. Mere sticks in the distance, they ran barrows up and down ramps, hove upon pulleys from which buckets hung, or swung rhythmically with their picks. It was to this trench that the rats would be diverted from the intercepting sewers and along it that they would run, straight for the circular trap, 2,000 yards in circumference, that had been prepared for them. The perimeter of the trap was formed from buried kegs of Linus Lucas's mixture; radii, also composed of kegs, divided it into sectors which would be detonated in succession over a period of several hours. I scribbled impressions of Rimmer conferring with Bazalgette

147

near the sewer outfall pumping station which was to be our ground headquarters, estimating its safety from the blast; of Owen and Lucas debating the fusing of the barrels and, behind them, squads of Artillerymen paying out electric cables and burying them; of Meredith Blake and Mossop assembling the *Gloriana*; and, the last sketch of all, of Crashaw as he stood alone in the centre of the trap, surveying the freshly dug trench, the powder emplacements, the detonating points, and the observation post. One of his staff had told me that the colonel had not slept or eaten throughout the period of preparation, that he had not stopped in one place longer than thirty minutes and had not sat down for longer than five; the strain was depicted in his face as I drew it, the flesh puffy, the eyes reddened, deep stains above the cheek-bones and ashen pallor below. I dated the drawing 31 December, noon. One hour before the attack began.

Of the happenings in the last twelve hours of the year 1863 I myself can tell only in part. On Rimmer's suggestion, however, I acquired accounts from the other members of Yelverton's Committee: from Owen, who joined Captain Hazard aboard the *Jupiter* on the Metropolitan Line; from McWhirrie, who elected to go with Crashaw's men into the sewers; from Gunn, who joined the raid upon the Hungerford Warren; from Bazalgette, who stationed himself at the junction of the intercepting sewers at Old Ford in Hackney; and from Pride and Passion, who attached herself to the Army doctors stationed at the sewer exits. Pieced together, their accounts reveal the course of events that led to the Battle of Barking Marsh.

It was with no little trepidation, said Richard Owen, that I peered through a slit in the plating, as our iron-clad train left the sheds of King's Cross at noon, and saw the tunnel of the Metropolitan Line grow larger as we swayed towards it. I had joined Captain Hazard at the controls of the engine but was unable to share his youthful enthusiasm for the venture, or his sanguine predictions of its outcome. Our progress seemed lamentably slow; the train, made cumbersome by its plating, responded sluggishly to Hazard's direction; and I feared that any irregularity in the rails might wreck us and leave us at the mercy of our enemies. The blackness of the tunnel closed around us. As my eyes became accustomed to the nigritude, I looked ahead and was horrified by what I saw. The floor of the tunnel and the track itself were covered by huddling, jostling packs of rats, each accompanied by one of the giants that we have come to know as war-lords. Captain Hazard, however, was undismayed.

'Time,' he said, 'for my first little modification.'

He operated a lever and brought down in front of the boiler a metal contraption like an extended, inverted grass-rake, not dissimilar to the American cowcatcher. The implement drove the rats before us, crushing some, thrusting others aside, forcing the packs to retreat. They re-formed, however, and mounted the sides of the train, attempting to force an entrance through the gun embrasures.

'Steady as she goes!' cried Hazard and, spinning a wheel, released a fierce emission of steam from a pipe that he had constructed along the length of the train, scalding the rats and forcing them to relinquish their position. He blew the engine's whistle, the signal for our gunners to open fire. Smoke balls exploded ahead of us, and when we had passed through the black curtain, we found that the line was clear for many yards ahead, that the rats were in flight.

We met little further opposition until we approached Baker Street station. Hazard had retracted our cowcatcher and extended before us a massive metal shield. Increasing our speed to its maximum, he advanced towards the wreckage strewn near the station and forced it from the track, so that it piled high over the platform. More rats had been concealed behind the debris; had we halted to clear the line, they would have caught us in a deadly ambush; as it was, our shield cleared them as efficiently as our cow-catcher, and our smoke balls put them to flight once more. This was their last stand. When we steamed into Paddington station, it was deserted. Our assault upon the Metropolitan Line had proved victorious. It was three o'clock when we disembarked and signalled the news to Crashaw at Barking.

We went down into the sewers in force as noon struck,

recounted McWhirrie. The soldiers wore smocks of tarpaulin and long boots. They moved deliberately, halting at each gully and drain to fire cartridges into every aperture. Two men doubled into each branch; they were armed with canisters, fused for delayed action, and tossed them as far as they could. I had joined the contingent which had been allotted the Covent Garden sewer, since its course was familiar to me from Rimmer's descriptions. As before, the rats hid at the onset, but thirty minutes later we heard the cry of a war-lord; we guessed that they were preparing to attack and took our prescribed precautionary measures. Each contingent had been equipped with a modified three-pounder; four men had manhandled ours without any great love through the manhole and around each twist of the sewer. Now it proved its value: the four gunners assembled it, brought it up to the front and fired large smoke balls from it; they achieved its full range along the straight stretches but covered almost as much ground in the winding sections by carefully judged ricochets. In this way we held off the rats when they launched their frontal attack; the screen of smoke that we had left behind us discouraged them from making a simultaneous assault from the rear. By now, however, the smoke and fumes were so dense that they threatened to overwhelm the men; the order to don our charcoal-packed masks was given; and, thus protected, we completed our run to the lower exit of the sewer and withdrew in good order, although several men suffered afterwards from the effect of the smoke. It was five o'clock when we signalled the successful completion of our exercise to the Rifles' command post, whence it was relayed to Crashaw at Barking.

I visited several of the field dressing stations established at the exits of the sewers, Pride and Passion told me, and was terribly alarmed at the awful condition of some of the men when they ultimately emerged. A few were horribly bitten; but many more had suffered frightfully from the smoke, some because they had been woefully slow to don their masks, others because the masks themselves were desperately primitive.

I wanted to see the results of our fumigation, continued

McWhirrie, and went to the Finsbury sewer that Maginn had explored. The soldiers had finished their run and, having rested, were re-forming to clean out any rats that had survived the smoke. They went in with fixed bayonets and poked and prodded into each orifice, dislodging and killing the living. I was shocked at the number of suffocated rats that lay in the branches and of those that had drowned in flight along the main channel. I am a naturalist, and frankly my love of animals exceeds my love of man. I was sickened by the slaughter for which we were responsible and at the thought of the massacre that we had planned at Barking Marsh. I reminded myself, however, that these were not naturally innocent creatures but monsters that had refined their worst instincts by the adoption of man's and were thus indistinguishable from the rabid or the rogue. Yet I longed to be back in Aberdeen or Orkney, where there were no dense settlements of men to corrupt and degrade the natural environment.

My family has bred soldiers for six generations, boasted Gunn; there was a Gunn, so I have discovered, at Agincourt. It is, therefore, unsurprising that my blood quickened at the inception of the raid upon the Hungerford warren in which I had the inestimable honour to participate. We assembled at the Westminster terminus of the experimental pneumatic tube by which our transportation to Hungerford was to be effected. So consuming was my excitement that I was impervious to any sensation of claustrophobia as I took my place next to Lieutenant Coker, the commander of our expedition, in the cylindrical casket, flattened at its base, by which we were to be conveyed; together we lay fully extended, our arms cruciform upon our chests. The lieutenant signalled his readiness and the automatic doors of the tube opened. As we entered, I experienced disagreeable sensations of pressure upon the ear and a chill draught upon the eyes, but once fairly within the tube, these adverse effects of suction were relieved, and the journey was subsequently marred only by the uneven motion of our conveyance and the odour of rust which assailed us. The engineers of the company, having studied plans annotated by

Rimmer, had calculated the amount of propulsion required to bring us to a point where the tube passed directly over the Hungerford sewer; when we reached it our casket was stopped, and we removed a plate from its base; the lieutenant penetrated the sewer below and we descended, while our casket was set in motion once more to give access to its successor.

Our expeditionary force numbered thirty, armed with smoke balls and cartridges, with live ammunition and bayonets. Lieutenant Coker divided it into three: an advance guard of seven, sixteen fumigators, and a rear guard. Without haste, smoke balls and cartridges were inserted in every hole and crevice, and canisters were lobbed into every subsidiary sewer. It was as we drew near to the 'nursery' of the warren that we were attacked. The war-lord sentinels took us in the front and rear, since we were not equipped with artillery to hold them at a distance. Lieutenant Coker, with admirable resolution, formed the advance and rear guards into two ranks and ordered them to respond alternately in the best Wellingtonian manner, standing and firing, kneeling and reloading. So determined was our resistance that the rats' attack faltered, whereupon we advanced with fixed bayonets and routed them. I observed, however, that it required several well-placed shots to eliminate each giant and that they survived a multitude of bayonet thrusts before they fell; moreover, even in the agonies of death, they fought on, snapping at the soldiers who forced a way past or over their prone bodies. At length, we entered the medieval chamber where Rimmer had seen the packs assemble; it was here that our raid achieved most, for the area was crammed with animals and our repeated volleys of smoke cartridges in the confined space rapidly overcame them. Suffering ourselves from the density of the smoke, we donned masks and retreated to the tube, where we inserted ourselves once more into the caskets, which had been dispatched at a prearranged time, and were conveyed to the northern terminus at Holborn. It was four o'clock when we signalled the successful outcome of our mission to Colonel Crashaw at Barking.

At noon, Bazalgette wrote, I occupied a sealed observation compartment at the junction of the Middle and High Level intercepting sewers at Old Ford; I looked down upon the penstock chamber, a great, arched passage in which the flow of sewage and storm water from the intercepting sewers is regulated and from which it is channelled into a huge, bisected sewer that carries it to the outfall at Barking Creek. I had no notion at what time the result of our fumigating operations would become apparent and passed the time checking and rechecking the signal lamp by which I would pass messages to the ground above. Three hours elapsed before I became aware of a sound that grew in volume and drowned the placid gurgle of the flowing sewage. I am not a literary man and cannot adequately describe it, save that it was the noise of a hundred beam-engines rising and falling as one; a thousand locomotives steaming abreast at full speed; ten thousand horses of the Heavy Brigade at the charge; a hundred thousand Maoris stamping in a war-dance. Metal plates in the walls of the chamber vibrated with its resonance, rivets started from their holes and girders quivered in their sockets. Then the first rats appeared: so densely were they massed that they filled entirely the lower part of the penstock passage; they ran along the upper walls too, defying gravity, outward pressure from the centre holding them in place; many were dead from suffocation or compression, but their corpses were carried along, wedged between the haunches of the living; war-lords and commoners ran together, the giants biting, clawing, and buffeting at their inferiors to force a passage past them. I signalled to the ground that they had come; it was three o'clock.

The first rats were, I guessed, from the eastward parishes, Hackney, Shoreditch, and Finsbury; towards five o'clock, however, I noticed that the fugitives were fatter, sleeker, and stronger, and assumed that they were from west and central London, where they lived well on the leavings of Westminster, Kensington, and Chelsea; I saw more war-lords, too, and wondered if they were from the Hungerford warren. By seven o'clock the procession had begun to

153

dwindle and I began to wonder how they had fared at Barking Marsh. I prayed that our calculations had been correct and our preparations without omission; for if we had erred in any way and the rats were to escape, then we should have let loose on London and the south-eastern counties a ravaging horde, bringing in its wake famine and pestilence. If we had failed, then to 1348, the Year of the Black Death, and 1665, the Year of the Great Plague, would be added 1863, the Year of the Rats.

At noon, Rimmer, Crashaw and I were in position at our headquarters, the pumping station on Barking Creek. Mossop and his Artillerymen, having unshipped *Gloriana*, began to inflate her bag. Blake scuttled around them, loudly bewailing their ineptitude and threatening sanguinary reprisals if one inch of silk were torn. Rimmer and Crashaw, who had achieved a tacit truce, discussed the signalling procedure agreed with our heliographers in London and regarded with dismay the cramped accommodation of *Gloriana*'s car.

'Be of good cheer,' Blake reassured them, exuberant now that *Gloriana* was swelling unharmed. 'Plenty of room for three.' And, he added, checking his inventory, for ballast equal to the weight of four; a battery of aneroid barometers and self-registering thermometers, telescopes, miner's lamps, heliographs, signalling lamps, waterproof capes, a hamper—'cold fowl, game pie, three cheeses, and some drinkable champagne'—and two portfolios of maps. In addition, there was a pile of shells with calico parachutes attached to them, which puzzled me when I looked into the car, until Rimmer explained that they were Boxer lights, constructed to float above the ground and illuminate it; much of the observation from the balloon, he reminded me, would be done after dark.

Mossop reported that *Gloriana* was ready for launching. Blake vaulted into the car and busied himself with ropes and anchors, while Rimmer persuaded Crashaw to allow the two of us to make the trial ascent. 'Hang it, we can't risk losing our C.-in-C. if this damned contraption bursts or soars off to the Pole.'

154

Crashaw succumbed to Rimmer's argument, not, I think, reluctantly; and Rimmer and I entered the car, to peer nervously over the edge while Blake made final adjustments to the anchors at bow and stern, jettisoned the first ballast and cast off. With a lurch and an awesome creaking of wicker and rope, we rose. Four minutes later we had reached 500 feet and I looked out over London from the clearest sky for a month. I traced the eastern parishes as on an architect's model, each square, each crescent, each warehouse and church as neat as if it had been modelled in papier-mâché; with the aid of Blake's telescope I looked westwards to the dials of the Westminster Clock and, beyond the metropolis, to the verdant fields and virid woodland of Middlesex and Essex emerging from the snow. Most beautiful of all, however, was the Thames, a tinsel streamer, striped by bridges and flecked by boats. I seized my sketch-book, forgetting rats, sewers and explosives in my desperation to fix with soft black lead on creamy paper all that I saw below. Blake spoke at my side. I heard the words 'death' and 'flight' and 'on such a day as this' but paid no heed; my mind was in my fingertips.

While I sketched, Rimmer operated the heliograph. First, he contacted each of our heliographers, checking the efficiency of the system; then he asked for situation reports which he transmitted to Crashaw below. Hazard had attacked along the Metropolitan Line; the Riflemen had entered the sewers; Coker was preparing his raid on thc Hungerford warren; and, as we heard the clock on Barking Church strike two, Coker had begun his attack. Rimmer ordered Blake to descend.

'The next signal should be from Bazalgette. Crashaw must be in position up here by then.'

We descended and bumped upon the ground. I disembarked, lost my legs, and sat down in a heap, Rimmer on top of me. By the time we had regained our balance, Crashaw had embarked; he leant from the car and spoke to Rimmer with something like amiability.

'The plan seems to be working.'

Rimmer responded with something like respect. 'I must

congratulate you on your organization and the vigour with which it has been accomplished. I didn't think that so much could have been achieved under one man's direction in two days.'

Crashaw hesitated. 'Rimmer—this is how I should have acted in the first place. I was irked at being entrusted with such a menial task, or so it seemed; and I was too stubborn to accept your criticisms and those of the others when I tried to find what seemed to be easy solutions to it. In consequence, I wasted sixty lives. I—I want you to know that in recognition of my guilt I have submitted my resignation today.'

Before Rimmer could reply, Crashaw gave the order to ascend and Blake cast off once more. As they rose swiftly above us, Rimmer shook his head.

'It may be a salve for his self-respect, but it won't atone for his crime.'

Linus Lucas, who had been engaged since our arrival in examining and checking the detonating systems, reported that the explosive was now being purified and would be ready for detonation in thirty minutes.

'Very good,' said Rimmer. 'Colonel Crashaw will signal as soon as the rats enter the diversionary trench. You will then allow fifteen minutes for the balloon to sail clear, before detonating the first sector of the trap.'

Lucas nodded and withdrew. We waited. At three o'clock Crashaw's heliograph flashed: the rats were at Old Ford. At four he signalled again: the raid on the Hungerford warren had been successful. At five o'clock the flashes once more.

'The last link in the chain,' said Rimmer. 'The rats have entered the diversion.'

Gloriana sailed westwards under the direction of her steam-powered propeller. We trained our glasses upon the point at which the diversionary trench entered the trap. At first we saw nothing; eventually, however, we noticed an irregular movement along the rim of the trench and realized that what we were seeing was the undulating back of the horde of rats, many layers deep, that was traversing its interior. Suddenly there was a spot in the centre of the trap,

156

barely distinct against the excavated earth; it swelled to a puddle that eddied into a pond that rippled into a lake that washed into a sea—a surging, tossing, foaming sea of rats.

It was a quarter past five; Lucas detonated the first sector.

A black flower bloomed in Barking Marsh with a force that shook the pumping station as if it had been a shack and sent a tremor under St Paul's; with a roar that made our noses bleed and drowned the Speaker at Westminster; with a blast that flung us against the pump-room wall and shattered windows all the way to Wapping. Fifteen minutes passed before the hail of mud and stones had diminished, the smoke thinned and the flames dispersed sufficiently, to allow us to see *Gloriana*. Crashaw was back over the trap and had dropped the first of his Boxers; he signalled that the rats were continuing to enter in force. We gave them fifteen minutes then blew the second sector.

By half past six the trap had refilled once more: we blew the third sector.

We blew the fourth at seven o'clock.

One sector was left, together with the trench which we had also packed with explosive. Bazalgette signalled that the flow of rats was decreasing and predicted that we should see the end of it shortly before nine o'clock; Crashaw ordered Lucas to blow the trench upon the hour. The rats streamed into the last sector; marsh gas, ignited by the explosion, burned around its perimeter and discouraged them from breaking out. We fired it at half past eight and directed our attention to the trench. Lucas was anxious: there was no way of knowing, he complained, if Bazalgette's prediction was accurate and if the last of the rats were coming into the trench now; he was loth to expend the remains of our explosive until he could be sure that it would account for the maximum number. The same thought had evidently occurred to Crashaw, for as we talked, we saw the balloon take up a position directly above the diversion, lose height until it was dangerously near the ground, and follow the line of the trench. Crashaw made 'Rats still coming' and repeated the signal ten minutes later. At five to nine he signalled that he was making a final check and dropped a Boxer light. At such a depth its parachute failed to open; the flare dropped into the trench and detonated the explosive. *Gloriana* and her crew were destroyed immediately.

We left Captain Mossop to supervise the remaining part of the operation—the liming and filling of the trench and crater, and the placing of traps and poison for any rats that had escaped—and descended to the hall of the pumping station. Yelverton had arrived, bringing with him Owen and Bazalgette. McWhirrie and Gunn appeared soon afterwards with Pride and Passion. Yelverton mixed congratulations upon the success of the operation with commiseration over the fate of Crashaw and Blake, and departed with hints that the Prime Minister and Another Personage would require a first-hand account of the Battle of Barking Marsh. Owen and Bazalgette stayed longer, and Pride and Passion brewed coffee which Rimmer laced secretly with rum. The conversation lapsed: our minds were upon Crashaw.

'I think that we did him an injustice, you know,' said Owen. 'He was misguided, perhaps, but very gallant.'

Bazalgette made an affirmatory noise in his throat and Pride and Passion echoed softly, 'Very gallant.'

The clock on Barking Church struck eleven o'clock.

'Aweel,' said McWhirrie, 'mebbe ye shudna look for mair in a sojer.'

'He knew the disciplines of wars,' quoted Gunn, 'and there is an end.'

It was only when we were alone in our cab, on our way home to Little Newport Street, that Rimmer pronounced his epitaph on Crashaw.

'If this were a novelette, Matt, then Crashaw would have died a hero, just as those good people think. But, as I've told you before, this is no story: it's the reality of the nineteenth century.' He drew a heavy breath. 'The Boxer flares were carefully labelled, Matt, with the heights from which they should be dropped. I'll wager Crashaw ignored the label and killed himself and Blake through sheer stupidity.'

He cocked an ear, 'Hark!'

I listened with him. The bells of London were ringing in the New Year.

X
A king dances

The Home Department's diligent fingers tied the loose ends that our campaign had left trailing, knotting them so unobtrusively that the public was unaware of their existence. The newspapers agreed to confine themselves to a brief statement, that the inclemency of the weather had driven rats to seek food above ground in large numbers but that they had been efficiently exterminated by the Board of Works. Elsewhere in their pages, editors published a bulletin from the Board's Engineer, announcing the successful completion of tests upon a new method of underground fumigation; this explained, they added archly, the recent assumption of many Londoners, based upon clouds of smoke arising from manholes, that the Anti-Tobacco League had successfully driven the cigar and pipe smokers of the metropolis into subterranean reservations. Later issues carried an announcement from the Artillery Institution that methods of neutralizing explosives and of detonation had been the subject of experiments on Barking Marsh, and that compensation for damage from the resultant blast would be forthcoming to all who made written application with substantiating evidence. More discreetly, a series of flushings was inaugurated, to remove from the sewers the remains of rats that had been asphyxiated by smoke; and surveyors were sent to inspect the entire sewer system in order to ensure that the war-lords had been exterminated; within a week the flushers declared that the system was clear and the surveyors reported that every section of it, including the Hungerford warren, was free of war-lords. The marauding packs on the south bank were driven out by smoke and killed; the damage to the bridges at Blackfriars was attributed to accidental combustion and was repaired; and the Metropolitan Railway Company announced with pleasure that the flooding from the Fleet River, which had closed the line, had ceased, and reopened its stations.

If anyone read the obituaries of Colonel Augustus Crashaw, 'served with distinction in the Crimea—met his death while engaged upon experimental work with the Artillery—loved by his men . . .' and of Meredith Blake, '. . . man of science and explorer—courageous balloonist—accident above Barking . . .' and connected them, the fact was not reported to us. If anyone questioned the right of the Widow Scud to a pension that allowed her to return with her family to Ireland, we did not hear of it. And if comments were made upon the disappearance from society of Anthony Norris and the terse replies of the police and other authorities to enquiries concerning the same, they did not reach us. The resignation of Mr Ashley Durston from the Home Department also passed unremarked; if he was noticed or recognized by the English gentry who toured Italy in succeeding winters, no one then or since has published the fact in letter or journal.

Rimmer and I needed rest, we told ourselves, and took it. For three days after the Battle of Barking Marsh, we lay abed late, overate and consumed abundant quantities of port and brandy-and-water. When we did drag ourselves from the fleshpots, however, Rimmer would work upon the full and confidential report which Yelverton had demanded from him—'Written, if you please, in language suitable for the public archives, none of your journalistic verbiage'; while I prepared a series of drawings to accompany it—'clear and informative, mind, devoid of all Romantic embellishment'. McWhirrie and Gunn, too, were under orders to prepare detailed appendices and did so in their studies at Hammersmith, conveying insults on each other's style by means of Gunn's aunt, as she passed between them with trays of tea and scones.

On the fourth day after the battle, Yelverton sent us instructions to equip ourselves appropriately for a visit to Downing Street two days thence. Rimmer drew from a carpet

160

bag, stored on the top of the larder, a suit of antique cut, worn, he asserted, by his father on the occasion of George IV's visit to Edinburgh; he shook out the folds and, having in the process evicted a family of mice from their commodious town residence, summoned Pride and Passion to redecorate it. I was driven to a tailor's for the ignominy of a fitting—'Would the young gentleman wish to retain his original—er—clothing, or should we burn it?'. Gunn stared in bafflement at his four black suits, unable to decide which was blackest and best. McWhirrie refused to give up his tweeds, bonnet and plaid until less than sixty minutes before our interview, and only when Yelverton seemed likely to expire from apoplexy. Pride and Passion emerged from her wardrobe the perfect Du Maurier, prouder and more passionate than ever; with the result that when we were taken before Lord Palmerston, it was she to whom the Prime Minister directed most of his questions and she at whom he looked when the rest of us answered.

We met the Other Personage a week later under circumstances in which we did not, I feel, make a lasting impression upon Her Majesty. The only time at which her equerry, Colonel Ponsonby, could arrange an audience was during her journey from Windsor Castle to Osborne, following a brief visit to the capital to inspect her newly-delivered grandson. We were to be presented, therefore, on Windsor Station prior to her departure on the Great Western Railway. Richard Owen, who had been a favourite of the Queen and the Prince Consort, instructed us for days in court etiquette and rehearsed with us a concise narrative of our adventures. Our clothes underwent his rigorous inspection and when he commanded McWhirrie to send for his kilt—'Her Majesty takes much pleasure in your native garb'—the authority in his tone was such that McWhirrie humbly obeyed. We were marshalled on the platform at one o'clock upon the appointed day, under a dismal mass of cumulonimbus and a heavy shower of rain which so bedraggled us that a wag in the crowd explained loudly to his chum that we were late arrivals for the New Year Alms. The Queen arrived; the station master bowed and the company

161

directors scraped; then Ponsonby presented us, at which point the engine whistled and drowned his words. Her Majesty passed on graciously and Pride and Passion cried all the way back to Paddington.

The following day had been set aside for our return visit to the Hungerford warren to survey what we called the Mastodon's Pit. Owen sent a note regretting that he could not accompany us but urging us to make the descent nevertheless; he had heard that rain and thawing snow were causing the level of water in the lower sewer system to rise, and he was anxious that we should find the pit again and mark its location as accurately as possible, in case conditions should cause the excavation to be postponed for any length of time.

We met at Horseferry and, having previously arranged with Bazalgette that the sewer outlet should not be obstructed, entered from the river end; then we walked to the point at which the old sewer had been blocked. The height of the stream had risen noticeably and sewage and water lapped at our knees. As we stood before the barrier, Gunn produced one of his foolscap sheets; it contained, he said, a record of the closing of the sewer, but the information had not proved as easy to find as we had anticipated. There had been no mention of the incident in the official minutes of the Westminster Commissioners of Sewers and he had searched every other volume or document covering the year 1723 in vain. Only when he was on the point of giving up, had he found a sealed packet labelled 'Special meeting, 1723', and, having sought permission to open it, had discovered in it the answer to our mystery. He cleared his throat.

19 April 1723. This day the Commissioners in private session summoned before them Samuel Mold, labourer, and examined him upon a certain deposition made by him, concerning the sewer at Hungerford Market. In which the said Samuel did depone that he had heard divers cries and noises proceeding from the branches thereof and had ventured into them and had therein beheld many rats and nests of rats of great size; but that when they had seen him they did attack him and the said Samuel fled; and that, fearful lest the said rats should plague the city,

162

the said Samuel did make his deposition. Having examined the said deponent and finding him of sober and honest disposition, the Commissioners did decide unanimously that the said sewer be sealed at its lower end and did instruct the secretary of the said Commissioners to send masons to accomplish the work forthwith. And that the matter be treated with all secrecy, the Commissioners resolved that it be separately minuted and the cost of the work be unspecified in the accounts.

'So Sam stumbled on the Hungerford warren in its early days,' said Rimmer, 'and the sentinels nearly did for him. No wonder the commissioners erected a barrier.'

'But why did they keep it a secret?' I asked. 'If the authorities had known of it earlier, much needless suffering might have been prevented.'

'They kept it a secret,' Gunn explained, 'because the sewer was their responsibility and if they had admitted the presence of the war-lords, they would have had to pay for any damage caused by the rats and the cost of exterminating them.'

'Damned irresponsible, nevertheless,' sniffed Rimmer.

'I wudna say that,' McWhirrie rejoined mildly. 'If I'd been payin' sewer rates tae yon commissioners and foon' they needit double the sum tae keep doon the rats, I'd mebbe hae commended their discretion in haudin' their tongues. But then I'm fae Buchan an' we're aye carefu' o' oor pennies theer.'

We threaded the sewer, passed through the deserted nursery and crawled to the brink of the Mastodon's Pit. Water gleamed at its base, but we agreed to the descent and unshipped a rope-ladder from one of our knapsacks. I volunteered to go first and reached the bottom without difficulty, sinking into eighteen inches of mud. Gunn joined me, heated by the exercise and complaining bitterly at the smell, but McWhirrie plumped down beside him and wheeshed him to silence. Rimmer arrived, hung about with extra lanterns, and cursing the large box that McWhirrie had begged him to add to his burden. McWhirrie busied himself with the container while the rest of us peered at the walls by the augmented light of our bull's-eyes. We found the metacarpal; and, on summoning McWhirrie to view it, discovered that he had erected a tripod and camera and was inserting a glass plate. Gunn at once straightened his hat and Rimmer's hand flew to his whiskers, but McWhirrie ignored them and, ordering us to remain motionless, lit a magnesium flare and started to count while he made his exposure. As he prepared to take a second, Rimmer stood beside his meta-carpal, looking triumphant.

'Man,' growled McWhirrie, motioning him away, 'the photographic apparatus exists tae further science an' no' tae preserve fer posterity the gowkin' faces o' loons wi' tae high an opinion o' themselves.'

When the photography was finished to McWhirrie's satisfaction, Gunn revealed that he was anxious about the fate of the metacarpal; the water rising in the pit might wash away the soil that held it, he suggested, or an excavator descending the walls might inadvertently crush it. McWhirrie supported him and Rimmer acquiesced. Gunn produced materials that he had prepared for such an eventuality—'The imponderable nature of archaeological investigation renders such precautionary measures advisable'—and went to work. He enveloped the face of the bone in canvas strips dipped in plaster and, having allowed the covering to dry, eased the bone around and performed the same operation upon its other sides; when it was entirely covered, he inserted his fingers into the soil and withdrew the metacarpal in its casing, placing the white lump into a box lined with cotton waste.

'The case is still a trifle damp,' he told Rimmer.

'Then we must trust that the Mastodon was not rheumatic,' Rimmer replied.

There were no signs of other bones in the vicinity of the metacarpal, so when we had finished measuring, drawing, and mapping the stratification of the pit's walls, we ascended. Back in the warren, we continued eastwards, intending to leave via the entry into the Covent Garden sewer. We stopped in the medieval cellar to allow Gunn to make sketches of the vaulting and to search for mason's marks. As he moved from wall to wall, uttering cries of admiration, I

164

noticed that McWhirrie was prone upon the floor, which was awash to the depth of three inches, and it occurred to me that there were better places on which to rest. He summoned us all to his side, however, and pointed to a handful of droppings.

'They're recent,' he said.

I was back between lurid covers again, sensing impending doom and having sudden premonitions.

'War-lords?' asked Rimmer.

'Elders, mair like,' answered McWhirrie.

'So they didn't all perish,' murmured Gunn.

'And if they're left undisturbed to recuperate,' declared Rimmer, 'they'll breed again and the story will be repeated. We must go after them.'

No one dissented. We took an inventory of our arms and ammunition. We had all brought toshers' staves; in addition, Rimmer had six smoke balls and a knife, and McWhirrie had a *sgian dubh*. Not exactly the Woolwich Arsenal. I asked Rimmer where he thought the survivors might be; and he reminded me of our first visit to the cellar when we had seen the elders of the warren. Had I noticed, he asked, that they came from a direction opposite to that of the rat-packs that had assembled there. Perhaps they had a secret lair . . .

'Somewhere,' he mused, leading us to the far wall, 'near here.'

The wall was blank; there was a recess in it, like a small ambry at floor level, but that too offered no aperture. Gunn's response was to say 'Open Sesame!' in a hopeful way; and I was so attuned to novelettish themes that I thought there might be a secret passage, made accessible by a block on a spring. Rimmer provided a more mundane answer, however, by discovering at the base of the ambry, concealed by the overlap of the wall, a narrow vent.

'Who's to be first?' he asked.

The disadvantages of being small, light, and junior re-asserted themselves and, while the others piled our baggage on a platform of broken masonry, I entered the vent and slid down a passage like a coal chute, arriving at the bottom with the same grace as a sack of best Durham. Before me opened a tunnel, with an inverted base and flattened top, built of flattened pink bricks. A sack of Rimmer joined me and confirmed my immediate impression, that we confronted what had once been an open channel, subsequently roofed over. Deliveries of Gunn and McWhirrie followed, the former having left a number of buttons and patches of skin at the entrance to the chute. It was he who now took the lead, glancing briefly at the tunnel and exclaiming: 'By Jove, what a find! My word, what a discovery!' before darting into it and progressing as fast as his knees would carry him.

'Fit is he bletherin' aboot?' asked McWhirrie and pursued the enthusing antiquarian, demanding enlightenment.

From fifty yards ahead Gunn's voice reached us. 'Great chasm in the floor here, twenty yards across, deep too. We'll need the ladder.'

'Wul ye no' haud still an' tell us fit it is ye've foon'?' pleaded McWhirrie, joining him.

'Certainly,' said Gunn, turning his back upon the chasm. 'The brickwork, the construction, it's quite obvious . . .'

But the obvious was not stated. Two elders sprang from the shadows of the wall and bore McWhirrie and Gunn backwards into the chasm. Even as we raced to its edge, a further section of the floor collapsed, falling in upon their bodies, filling up their grave to a depth of many feet.

'Go back!' cried Rimmer. 'Get help! I'll do what I can here.'

As I turned about, however, I saw that our retreat had been cut off. The bulk of an elder plugged the tunnel. We brought our staves forward, Agincourt fashion, and waited for him to spring, but he hesitated. We knew why, when a second emerged from the shadows behind Rimmer. We knelt back to back. As I did so, I felt Rimmer scrabbling in his pockets and something was pushed into my hand: it was a smoke ball, its fuse fizzing. We threw our missiles together and charged our opponents while the smoke blinded them. I took mine in the breast and withdrew my stave in time to lance him again as he threshed in agony. Hearing Rimmer call, I spun around, to find him prostrate, his stave broken and the elder upon his back, thrusting with his muzzle at

Rimmer's neck-guard. I jabbed him in the haunches but he would not slacken his hold; reversing my grip, I hammered on his neck until he swung his head towards me, whereupon I drove my stave straight at him with all my weight behind it and spitted him between the eyes. I levered the beast from Rimmer's back but my companion was unconscious; there was blood on his scalp and the angle of his arm and shoulder seemed unnatural.

I squatted, retrieving my wind, and thought how unbelievable it was, that, with the Battle of Barking Marsh a victory, and the war against the rats won, two men had died and another had been severely injured, while I myself was alone and a prey to any elder who cared to attack. It is indicative of my self-pity at this moment that I neither dredged up another cliché from the novelette nor fainted—my customary responses to ill-fortune—but simply declared like a sulky child, 'T'ain't fair'. I regret to say that the victim of unfairness was not, to my mind, either of the dead men or the injured Rimmer: it was I.

'Inelegantly expressed, old chap, but I second your proposition.' Rimmer had regained consciousness and eyed me with amusement. 'Be that as it may, what are you going to do?'

'Fetch help, I suppose.'

'Don't. I view the water level in this tunnel with some suspicion. You would feel a frightful ass if you were to return with a stretcher and hoist to find me under a foot of diluted sewage; and I don't suppose I should feel too brisk about it either. No, you're going to have to do something heroic, my dear fellow—and not before time—without any help whatsoever from me, I'm afraid; that brute seems to have buckled a variety of ribs and my collarbone has gone in search of a better position. Don't let me detain you.' With that, he lost consciousness once more.

His mocking tone had precisely the effect he had intended; it jolted me out of self-pity and into annoyance. I stripped off my coat and put it under his head, transferred the contents of his pockets to my trousers, picked up my stave and the remains of his, and went back to the coal chute. Lacking claws and muscular haunches, I made slow work of the ascent and had to drop both staves before I finally pulled myself out on my elbows. I poked my head from the ambry and withdrew it sharply when I saw three elders nosing our pile of baggage. I extracted one of Rimmer's smoke balls and, praying that the wet floor would not extinguish it, tossed it into the knot around the knapsacks. As the elders dispersed in the smoke, I charged towards the baggage, seized it on the run, subsequently dropped three of the bundles, and ended on top of the mound of rubble on the other side of the cellar with Gunn's knapsack and McWhirrie's camera. Ignoring the elders, I tugged and hauled at chunks of masonry until I had built a rampart around me; behind it I amassed a pile of stone fragments and laid out the contents of my pockets and the knapsack. There were Rimmer's remaining smoke balls and his knife; some canvas strips which Gunn had not used when encasing the metacarpal; an empty, stoppered jar in which he had carried the plaster; a bottle of port (a nice thought of his, that) and a flask of eau-de-Cologne; left in the knapsack were the encased metacarpal and a heavy tome on excavation. Only when I had laid these to hand, did I peer over my wall at the enemy. The three elders had spread out and were coming vengefully towards me, bellies arched, muzzles distended, tails whipping. They were old and infirm, these Wise Men of the warren, but they looked a formidable enemy as they approached the foot of my fortress.

There was no point in keeping the brutes at a distance; that would simply postpone the issue and I did not know for how long Rimmer could be left without attention. An idea had come to me, however, as I had been taking stock of my arsenal, and I decided to risk it; it was based upon an engraving I had cut of a sketch made during the revolution in Poland, when the rebels had manufactured their own bombs on the barricades. Discouraging the elders from coming too close, by pelting them at intervals with my stone fragments, I toasted Gunn in a swig of his port, then divided the rest equally between the bottle, the jar, and the flask; I took the canvas strips and stuffed them into my three containers, saturating them in the wine; I hacked the fuses from three of the smoke balls and, cutting or chipping holes in the stoppers of the containers, inserted a fuse into each; then I waited for the rats to come within range.

They were clawing their way up the rubble, one taking me from the left, one from the right, one advancing in the centre. I knew that I must pick them off singly, before they could make a concerted attack. I chose the one on the left for my first target; he was the fastest and looked the most powerful. I lit the fuse that dangled from the port bottle and tossed it to the beast's feet; he extended an enquiring muzzle and at that moment the bottle exploded; flames rippled along his old, dry coat and he rolled, a blazing mass, to the floor. The other two increased their speed when they beheld the fate of their fellow. I dealt next with the one on the right, using the plaster jar, and achieved the same success. In the churchyard at St Pancras I had seen a young war-lord fight on even when badly burned, but the elders were too frail to survive the pain and shock. I faced my third opponent, who had come uncomfortably close; I tossed the cologne flask before him but he patted it with his foot and it clattered down the mound to explode harmlessly at the bottom. The rat reared up on the rampart and I reached for the only missile to hand: Gunn's tome on excavation. I hurled it at his head, upset his balance so that he fell backwards and, leaping after him, drove my knife into his throat.

I rose to my feet. The anger which Rimmer had inspired, and which had given me the resolution to defeat my opponents, evanesced, leaving me shaking and vomiting at the smell of blood and burnt meat. When the fit was over, I retrieved Gunn's knapsack, the metacarpal still intact, and McWhirrie's box of photographic apparatus, and surveyed the cellar, mentally calculating our toll of the elders: two in the chasm, two in the tunnel, three here—seven. I reminded myself of our first visit to the cellar, imagined that I could see the elders entering, and counted—nine. One had perished the same day; one, therefore, might still be alive. He was. Behind me.

Seeing him, I felt as I had felt when the Volunteers had died in the sewer and I had thought that I could not escape: a

169

tranquility, a relief that the suspense and fear were at an end. There was no strength left in me and I sat on McWhirrie's box with a foolish grin on my face, while the beast circled me, each revolution bringing him nearer, until the stench of his body was in my nostrils. I could at least photograph him, I thought, and giggled as I pictured myself setting up the tripod, focussing the lens and firing the flash. The flash! I sprang to my feet, tore open the box, wrenched out the flash plate, magnesium wire coiled upon it, ready for use, and struck a match. The flare ignited and I thrust it at the muzzle that was less than a yard from me; the magnesium burned briefly, but long enough to singe my eyebrows and frighten the rat. As he retreated, I drew out the tripod, unfolded its foremost, spiked leg, and charged after him until his back touched the opposite wall; as he reared, at bay, I drove my makeshift bayonet into his breast and his reeking blood gushed over me. I staggered back and collapsed upon the flags.

The rat lay huddled at the foot of the wall for several minutes. At length, he summoned his remaining strength and struggled to his feet; he made another effort and hauled himself upon his hind legs. He paid no attention to me; his eyes were blank; only his ears twitched, as if he could hear something that I could not. He tottered in a circle, his feet forming a jerky, wavering pattern. Only then did I realize that his movements were not the uncontrolled responses of an animal maddened by pain; they were deliberate; they were precise. The giant rat was dancing. And I remembered the broadsheet, *Brave News from Hungerford*:

It will . . . perform a Dance of Grace and Intricacy upon its Hinder Legs . . .

And I knew that I beheld no elder but the king of the warren, king, indeed, of London-under-the-ground. This was the heir, the last of the line, of Rattus Rex, and he was performing in his death throes the quaint measure that had descended in memory from his royal ancestor. And though I stank with his blood and had rejoiced in the extermination of his loathsome race, yet the sight of his stepping feet, his arms

170

upstretched like a child's, so moved me that I wept. As I covered my eyes, I heard for the last time the war-lord's call and saw his body collapse; his tail twitched once and then no more. Rattus Rex was dead.

I made my way back to Rimmer, first tossing into the chute the remains of our baggage, and, sliding down after it, recovered the staves that I had lost in my ascent. Rimmer gave me a weak grin of welcome when I appeared, but I saw that his pain was severe and that he eyed the rising water-level with apprehension. Had I, he enquired, when I had summarized my adventures, thought of a means by which we might escape? I said that I had, and proceeded to construct it. Once again, I drew upon memories of blocks that I had engraved, this time a sketch of Red Indians on the move. From my stave and the two pieces—one long, one short—into which Rimmer's had broken, I constructed a roughly isoceles triangle, binding the corners with rope from the ladder. Across this frame I stretched sections of the ladder to form a mesh; and to the mesh I strapped Rimmer, or as much of him as would fit. He now rode in a sort of horse-sledge, while I took the part of the horse. I knew that I could not transport him up the chute and he was in no condition to cross the chasm, so I decided to take the third route available to us—if, indeed, it existed—and dragged him towards the shadowed aperture from which the elders had ambushed us.

Much as I admire Lord Tennyson, I have never had the privilege of meeting him, which is a great loss for both of us, since my journey along the pipe to which the aperture led— tunnel is too grand a name for it—could only be described fittingly by his pen; he has thus been deprived of an epic and I of a bard. The only illustration that I have discovered which bears the least resemblance to our manner of progress is in one of the Blue Books on Child Labour; it shows a spindly mite crawling on all fours along a narrow gallery in a coal-mine, dragging a loaded truck behind him. Rimmer, however, weighed more than a truckload of coal, and the pipe was the narrowest of the passages we had attempted in the course of our underground adventures; only the impossibility of turning kept me from giving up. Rimmer remained in high good humour; or so I thought until I listened to his flow of chatter and realized that he was delirious. I dragged myself forward, water above my wrists and ankles and splashing my face at each step. After fifty minutes of jerking and jolting, two or three inches at a time, I fancied that the tunnel was widening; I refused to believe it, lest I be disappointed, and butted on. Fifteen minutes later I allowed myself to stop and measure, and to my joy found that I was correct. Although the pipe had grown steeper, its roof was higher, its walls were further apart. Soon I was kneeling, then crouching, then bending, until finally I reached my full height and hit my head on a metal disc in the roof; it was the cover of a manhole. I pushed it, it gave; I pressed harder, it rose; I gave a final thrust and it opened. I hauled myself into its mouth and stared at a high, vaulted ceiling above me; at a policeman, who dropped his truncheon; at a clerk, who dropped his files; and at a workman, who dropped his sandwiches. It was time for my last dip into the novelette.

'Where am I?' I asked.

'You're in the vaults,' said the policeman.

'Which vaults?' I asked.

'The 'ouse vaults, o' course,' said the workman.

'Which house?' I asked.

'The House of Lords,' said the clerk. 'And I'll trouble you to explain your presence.'

It makes sense when you look at Bazalgette's portfolios of plans. When they rebuilt the Houses of Parliament, they added new drains, utilizing existing courses, digging new. Since the Westminster Commissioners had sealed off the Hungerford sewer, however, the engineers and architects had forgotten about the drains extending from it, and had inadvertently linked the drains of the new Parliament buildings with some of the oldest in Westminster. The oldest and the most dangerous. As Rimmer said, 'If you could pop up in the House of Lords so easily, it's a wonder the rats didn't.' He mused, remembering Yelverton, and added, 'It's not a wonder, it's a pity.'

I emerged from my hole. Rimmer came out from his

coma. McWhirrie and Gunn returned from the dead. Or so it seemed to me. For no sooner had I been given brandy, blankets and a dozen Parliamentary messengers, and informed the authorities of the death of our friends, than they arrived at the House, slightly put out at having organized in vain an expedition to retrieve our own corpses. It seemed to me a miracle equivalent to that of Lazarus but they modestly demurred.

'The essential feature of our narrative is that the tunnel into which we descended from the medieval cellar was a Hadrianic conduit,' said Gunn.

'It wis a Roman drain,' explained McWhirrie. 'An' it connectit wi' some Roman baths . . .'

'Smaller than those found in the Strand, but built on several levels. Thus, when we were propelled into the chasm . . .'

'We landit wi' a bump, but nae banes braken, further doon in the baths. Ma rat had smashed his skull an' I stabbed Gunn's wi' ma *sgian dubh* . . .'

'I was about to slay it with my stave. Then we crawled into a transverse conduit just as the earthfall blocked the chasm . . .'

'We jist crawled aboot efter that, till we cam' oot deep in the embankment workings and set aff tae meet ye . . .'

'But, finding to our dismay that you had failed to emerge at the appointed location, we expressed fears as to your well-being . . .'

'We thocht ye wis deid.'

I told Gunn that the metacarpal had survived, thanks to his meticulous treatment; and I described the death of the king of the warren. They fell silent until McWhirrie sighed and said, 'Theer wis mebbe nobility theer an' we were sae affeart we didna see it. Ach, I'm awa' back tae Aberdeen.'

We had one last meeting before our allies departed. Gunn's aunt spread a banquet before us, and we toasted each other in wine from Clapperton's store—all except Rimmer who sipped sulkily at beef tea.

'It's been the most eventful month of my not uneventful life,' he declared.

'Agreed,' said Bazalgette, 'but I'm glad it's over.'

'A safe seat in the Bodleian for me,' announced Gunn; then added wistfully, 'but I did enjoy the battle.'

'I've learned,' said Owen, 'how narrow is the line that separates coexistence and conflict between men and animals.'

'Aweel, mebbe,' said McWhirrie, which we took for assent.

We toasted absent friends and thought of Scud and Durston, of Crashaw and Blake, and—yes, why not, of Rattus Rex. Then Pride and Passion drank to the future. And that, I thought, was disturbing.

It disturbed me because she seemed to be spending daily more time at Rimmer's bedside and less in her dispensary, a situation which his condition barely justified. What was worse, Rimmer, swallowing her soup, her custards and her medicine, did not seem to object to her company. One afternoon, a fortnight after McWhirrie had departed for Aberdeen and Gunn for Oxford, I heard Pride and Passion talking softly to Rimmer as he pottered about his bedroom in his plaster casing.

'Of course, this place is quite unsuitable for you. You need a study, a library, a laboratory, even a wine-cellar, room to entertain people who can help you. You should look for a house in Kensington, Hampstead perhaps.'

'Mmm,' agreed Rimmer, 'then Matt could have his own studio.'

'I have been meaning to talk to you about Mathew,' said Pride and Passion . . . and I crept away, dreading what I might hear.

That evening, after she had left, Rimmer toyed with *Punch*, while I poked aimlessly at the fire. He cleared his throat.

'Er—Matt—er—Pride and—that is—Miss Tiptree—and I have been talking of certain matters—er—they included you—and—er—the upshot is . . .' He broke off. I jabbed at the fire and would not look at him. 'The upshot is—that I have here a telegram from McWhirrie, inviting us to Orkney to excavate a fort he has found; and I think we ought to accept before that damned woman interferes any further. Get down *Bradshaw*, old chap, and find us a train that will be in Edinburgh before she knows we've gone.'

As our train steamed out of King's Cross early the following morning, Rimmer looked back at London and remarked, 'No one will ever hear the truth about Rattus Rex, you know. Yelverton will keep it an official secret.'

I nodded.

'Pity,' he said, 'it's a rattling good yarn.'

I groaned.

'It would make a good novelette,' he continued, 'forty years from now, when all the remaining participants are dead or past caring.'

I agreed.

'Trouble is, would anyone believe it?'